TO A "Dear Friend" & For
The Rev. Dr. Samuel C. McKinney
a
Pioneer — Trailblazer and friend
of the Struggle!

Civil Rights
Leader for the
Oppressed

your friend and brother

John L. Scott

6/15/14

Published in the United States by
Beckham Publications Group, Inc.
P.O. Box 4066, Silver Spring, MD 20914

ISBN: 978-0-9848243-1-1
Library of Congress Cataloging in Publication:

Civil Rights Leader for the Oppressed

The Story of Rev. John L. Scott

JOHN L. SCOTT
WITH DR. BARBARA E. ADAMS

Foreword by Rev. Harold A. Carter, D.M., Ph.D.

Beckham
PUBLICATIONS GROUP, INC.

Silver Spring

Praise for *Civil Rights Leader for the Oppressed*!

John Scott has been an extraordinary and important preacher activist since the 1960s. His writings are undeniably an important addition to anyone's development and understanding of the Black church and the Civil Rights movement.

– Reverend Al Sharpton, **President & Founder, National Action Network**

As the major events in the Civil Rights Movement begin to fade from memory, Dr. Scott's detailed account of his childhood struggles in the segregated South, the names and places which inspired him to fight for the equality and justice and the remarkable assortment of courageous men and women who gave their lives to make democracy a reality, reminds us of the extraordinary high cost of freedom and some of the foot soldiers, known and unknown, who have led us "thus far on our way."

– Dr. James A Forbes, Jr
Pastor Emeritus of the Riverside Church, New York , NY
and the Founder and President of the Healing the Nations Foundation
and
the Harry Emerson Fosdick Distinguished Professor at Union

Reverend John Scott was there! He was an eye witness and direct participant in the struggle for human rights.

– Reverend Dr. Calvin O. Butts, III – Pastor, The Abyssinian Baptist Church In the City of New York

DEDICATION

To my father, the late Cofield Scott, trend-setting farmer, forever the visionary leader of the Quankey Community;

To my mother, the late Helen Jones-Scott, his helpmate, partner and dreamer of a better day for our people and their five sons;

To the late Rev. Dr. William A Jones, Jr., former pastor of the Bethany Baptist Church, Brooklyn, N.Y.; mentor, fellow co-worker and drum major for justice also known as the *Son of Thunder*;

To my wife Minnie, mother of our three sons who has given her best to our children to become leaders in their own right;

To John, Jr., J.D., my oldest son, first law graduate and law partner in the Scott family;

To James Augustine, my middle son, M.D., Obstetrics and Gynecology in the tradition of his great, great grandfather, Dr. Unug Jackson Scott;

To Jerome, my youngest and most gifted of his brothers,

And above all, to the Glory and Honor of God who let me live and gave me grace and the zeal to persevere. All praise and Glory unto God.

ACKNOWLEDGMENTS

Rev. Dr. Harold A. Carter, Rev. Dr. Wyatt Tee Walker, Rev. Dr. James A. Forbes, Rev. Bailey, Rev. Jesse Jackson, Sr., Rev. W. A. (Bill) Jones, Rev. Al Sharpton, Jr., Dr. J. Pius Barbour, Dr. Jesse Casterlowe, Dr. Moses Newsome, Carlos Brown, Augustus (Gus) Chavis, George Hall, Ed Weeks, Rev. Dr. Y.B. Williams, Dr. Carlyle Marney, the Cofields of Enfield, North Carolina, Rev. J.A. Felton, George Hall, Sr., Rev. S. P. Petteway, Rev. Herbert Daughtry, Rev. L. P. Taylor, Rev. Freddie Brunswick, Clayton Jones, Ben Wright, Percy Sutton, Earl Lewis, Dick Cavett, Gil Noble, Adam Clayton Powell, Jr., Rev. Abernathy, Rev. Carl Flemister, the Houdins of France, Deacon Bembry, Philmore Williams, Rev. Harvey Johnson, Rev. C. W. Cuffee, R. Preston Tisch, Alice White, Herbert Greene, Gwen Jones, Katie Hicks, Deacon Alexander McMillan, Gwen Crenshaw, Ruby Duncan, Rev. Clarence Grant, Rev. Bishop Norman Quick, Rev. Patricia Rheburg, Bishop Paul Moore, Rev. Youngblood, Ossie Davis, Rev. Wendell Foster, Rev. Calvin O. Butts, Rev. Richard Watkins, Rev. S. Frank Emmanuel, Rev. Robert Johnson, Hazel O, Reilly, Father Earl Koopercamp, Father Thomas Fenlon, Stanley Michaels, Commissioner William Bratton, Rev. Preston Washington, Adrian Lewis, editor; Wendell McArthur, book jacket photographer, St. John Baptist Church photographer and Allen Morgan. Photography contributed by Scott Archives. Gratitude to Dave and staff of Jacob Restaurant in Harlem.

FOREWORD

It is a good thing that John Scott, preacher, pastor, scholar, civil rights leader and family member has paused to put on paper his extensive experiences in the period of African American history that has seen such change over the last fifty plus years.

Considering that in these last fifty-plus years the history of African Americans in American, the white dominant culture life has moved from the stronghold of Jim Crowism, sharecropping on farms and women domestics riding in the backseats of their employers' cars to active demonstrations to protest against unjust and evil social practices and legislations that extend even to the present age, it was a very active time of change in African-American history. Now the promise of democracy is not only realized in the books, but the hearts and practices of the people and is still working to keep the dream of full citizenship for all God's people, wanting.

The one institution in the African-American community that pulled me and John Scott together was the magnet of the Christian Church. He was born and grew up on a farm in the northern community of North Carolina where his parents were landowners and prosperous farmers. As a result he grew up knowing the impoverished livelihood of Black farmers and the power of the Church in their lives.

On the other hand, I was born and grew up in Selma, Alabama in the heart of the Black Belt. My parents were Christian ministers and I was exposed to the plight of the Black family both in rural and city life. Both of us grew up in families where our parents instilled in us the vision of a better life for our people. We were both grounded in the need for disciplining ourselves in hard work, education, and the practice and growth in our faith. Because of this influence in our lives we met and became friends through our attendance at the Crozer Theological Seminary in Chester, Pennsylvania which is the theological school that nurtured Dr. Martin Luther King, Jr.

This was the school, with its liberal interpretation of biblical thought and strong emphasis on social and political justice for all God's people that helped to shape and nurture the mind and life of John Scott. This was the place where he was able to marry the fervor and faith of his education in the rural church of his native North Carolina with the models of social protest and civic change he learned from the Civil Rights Movement, especially as led by Dr. Martin Luther King, Jr.

There is one significant aspect of John Scott's involvement in this movement worthy of note. His primary motivation for being a foot soldier in the freedom fight struggle, especially that of being a voice for poor people, was his deep and abiding faith in Jesus Christ as Savior and Lord of his life. Trying to understand John Scott apart from the church and the gospel of Jesus Christ is absolutely impossible.

Personally, I was blessed to conduct revival services for John Scott when he pastured his first church, New Ahoskie Baptist Church in Ahoskie, North Carolina from1967 to 1969. I had been involved with him in non-violent civic protests in New York where we camped out in front of the A & P Headquarters, on the 9th floor of their corporate offices. We did fully prepare to go to jail, fighting for ordinary workers in this corporation for them to receive fair wages and employee benefits. This movement, led by the late Dr. William A. Jones, Jr., was a strong regional movement in Brooklyn, New York which in fact was another vital satellite of the broad-based Civil Rights Movement.

The fact that John Scott has served the great St. John Baptist Church, one of New York's leading churches for thirty-nine years, and has served as moderator of the United Missionary Baptist Association of New York is another testament to this strong courageous leadership from behind the pulpit to the marketplaces of life.

We recently walked down Fifth Avenue in New York City when we passed by a panhandler seeking money. John Scott walked about ten feet ahead of the person before he stopped and gave the individual a financial donation. As we walked away he stated, "I just don't care what people say, I simply cannot pass by anyone in need!" Sometimes, it is the *small things* in life that reveal the deep reservoir of love and compassion in a person's character.

One will see in reading this book that John Scott is ever driven by his creed. It flows in his family life and his love for his wife, Minnie Scott and their sons, all of whom have become productive and professional citizens serving the commonwealth of our times. A reservoir of love and compassion dwells in him in such a way that family and people of all races and across all classes are blessed because such a selfless and giving person exists among us. The spirit of love and dwelling in him will not permit him to ignore or deny the angelic nature of his deeper self.

Rev. Dr. Harold A. Carter
Crozer Alumnus & Schoolmate
New Shiloh Baptist Church
Baltimore, Maryland
February, 2012

INTRODUCTION

How This Book Became a Reality

I met Rev. John Scott, Pastor of St. John's Baptist Church for the first time in the early spring of 1980. It was shortly after I interviewed for the position of the Director of Social Services for the Wilson Major Morris Community Center. The Center was operated under the auspices of the church and meeting Rev. Scott concluded the interview process.

I immediately liked Rev. Scott. Prior to my interview, I never worked with a minister and had no idea what working with a Baptist minister would be like. In other words I had no expectations so the minister I met was a pleasant surprise. I remember he appeared very organized, upbeat and chatty; sort of bubbly and wanted to know about my background at the moment of our meeting.

I worked at Wilson Major Morris for one year and during my tenure, remained surprised at the level of energy and volume of work that was generated by a relatively young organization. Many useful, successful and viable programs came to fruition during this period, namely: the Nutrition Programs for Senior Citizens that fed nearly one hundred seniors daily, the Meals on Wheels Program, Housing, Transportation and Summer Youth Programs.

After I moved on, I periodically saw Rev. Scott in the Harlem Community and he always stopped to chat and request an update on what I was doing. In 1990, after I authored the first book on Dr. John Henrik Clarke I reached out to Rev. Scott to host a book signing and have Dr. Clarke speak at his church. He gladly obliged. Following that occasion and during the following years, I saw Rev. Scott in the Village of Harlem about once annually.

Imagine my total surprise in December 2010 when I returned to my office where I was the Director of the Rosa Parks Campus at the College of New Rochelle, to find him waiting to see me. Due to it being the Christmas season, I assumed that Rev. Scott stopped by to wish me season's greetings. However, when I jokingly asked if he was there to offer me a job, his answer was yes.

Then Rev. Scott shared with me that the encouragement and motivation for his book about his civil rights movement experience and success as a Harlem minister came from Rev. Keith Russell. He said after giving it some thought, that he considered approaching me to be his co–author. Of course I accepted and agreed to meet with him beginning January 2011. From the first meeting, we met weekly and vigorously worked on the project through August 2012.

I must say that Rev. Scott was organized from the very beginning, arriving with his outline and rough draft. As I have no knowledge of Southern culture I found reading his in-depth information on the South refreshing and hard to put down. I felt myself immediately emerged into the midst of an instant history lesson and learned so much. For example, I learned that businessman and philanthropist Julius Rosenwald, owner of Sears and Roebuck, not only donated money to Tuskegee Institute and permitted Booker T. Washington to use some of the funds for constructions purposes, he also built 5,500 two and three room elementary school houses for rural Black farming communities in North Carolina. Plus he influenced his friend George Eastman of the Eastman Kodak Company in Rochester, New York to build a premier high school for Black students in Enfield County in North Carolina. The memoir exposed me to counties and towns in North Carolina that I never knew existed such as Delmar, Enfield, Roanoke Rapids and Halifax County just to name a few, along with the painful integration process of these communities in and around the surrounding areas.

I continue to remain impressed that Rev. Scott has known the luminary Baptist ministers in the United States. He still communicates with ministers who are listed in the glossary of names especially Rev. Dr. Wyatt Tee Walker, Rev. Dr. Calvin O. Butts, Rev. Jesse Jackson, Rev. Al

Sharpton, Rev. W. Franklin Richardson, Rev. Dr. Harold A. Carter and Rev. Dr. James Forbes to name a few. Rev. Scott has a story to tell and it's certainly worthwhile documenting.

Dr. Barbara E. Adams
Harlem, New York
November, 2012

CONTENTS

CHAPTER ONE

EARLY BEGINNINGS

Historical Facts

As I look back over my life, I can only say that by the grace of God, "I've come this far by Faith, Leaning on the Lord, *Trusting* in His Holy Word." It has been an amazing journey all the way! It has been a "Miraculous Journey," because with my faith and trust in God, He made a way when it seemed like there was no way.

I grew up in the rural south in the entirely Black farming community of Delmar, Enfield, which is the oldest town in Halifax County, North Carolina. Several outstanding historical facts are associated with this community. It is the county seat is in Halifax County, North Carolina where the drafters of the Declaration of Independence met prior to meeting in Philadelphia, Pennsylvania, and drew up the "Halifax Resolves" (the rough draft of the Declaration of Independence, on June 12, 1776). Julius Rosenwald, the Chicago President of Sears and Roebuck Co., built 1,700 schools in North Carolina in the 1920s and the 1930s in Halifax County. This was more than in any of the other counties in North Carolina. Rosenwald also built a total of 5,500 schools in the South for *colored* people, as we were then called. Two and three room elementary school houses were located in each rural farming community, where Rosenwald influenced George Eastman of the Eastman Kodak Company in Rochester, New York to build a premier high school for the *coloreds* in Enfield. This premier high school became the Eastman High School where both my parents attended. A lady from Brooklyn by the name of Ms. Brick, established a premier college for our people on an 1100 acre tract of land and named it the *Brick Institute.* It was on par with Hampton and Tuskegee Institutes and this is where the economically privileged attended.

Introduction to the World

I was born a twin, and my brother and I were my parents' first children. I was named John meaning *Praise the Lord.* My middle name is Luster and I was the smaller and weaker twin. My twin brother's name was James Augustus and although he was bigger in size, he didn't live.

We were born in the home of our great uncle, Joe Jesse Jones, who was a well-to-do, outstanding and successful farmer as well as a World War I veteran. We were delivered by the midwife Mary Manley who was the popular midwife in the Enfield community.

My mother said that I was born dead and was Black and blue in color. So the midwife placed me over in a corner of the room, knelt down and began to pray over me. All of a sudden I began crying, kicking, hollering and never stopped.

Later in life, when I was about thirty years old, and announced my call to pastor in new Ahoskie, North Carolina, mother told me that she felt relieved for two reasons after Miss Manley delivered us and only one baby lived. She was relieved because she wondered how she was going to take care of two babies when she had never taken care of one and she couldn't possibly breast feed two babies. So at five months old, we were fed *Pet Milk*, the milk to which African-American babies were allergic. We were fed the milk without my parents knowing that it contained a solid that Blacks, Africans, South Americans and Mediterranean people didn't have the enzymes to properly digest its molecular structure. I learned this when my first son John Jr. was hospitalized at the age of six months because he was unable to digest milk.

19

My Parents

My parents came from the same community and in a way they were distant relatives. My mother was twenty-one and Daddy was twenty-three when they were married. They attended the same Rosenwald School and the same church. In the beginning, my mother's father was against the courtship because at thirteen Daddy quit school to run his father's farm. He wanted his father to pay him to work the farm and so he negotiated with his father to be paid. This was unheard of at that time. My mother's father felt that was disrespectful and he was clear in his opinion about this. Then he confronted my dad asking him why he was sneaking over to his place behind the woods to see his daughter. My father was brown skinned and because of the color prejudice then, Grandpa just didn't think my Dad was *light* enough.

Due to their already knowing each other from elementary and high school, my parents courted for a few months before a local preacher who was an organizer of the Holiness Movement married them. His name was Elder Joe Silver and he founded the Plum-Line Holy Church, in Hollister, North Carolina. He performed the ceremony. It was rumored that my parents ran away to be married even though they had a ceremony. I asked mother who said they didn't. However, one of my cousins said they did.

People can tell you a lot of stuff on the basis of shame when it's not the truth.

My mother's parents were the Joneses and they were also farmers. They were more average rank-and-file than my father's people, although my great-great grandfather (my mother's grandfather), along with seven other Black men purchased almost three thousand acres of land between them. This area became known as the *Delmar Tract*. Great-Grandfather Jones is buried in the family plot located in the church's cemetery of the Daniel's Chapel Baptist Church. He was the Chairman of the Deacon Board. After his death the chairmanship was passed down to his youngest son Boston Jones who is buried in the plot beside him.

Although my mother's ancestry was more outstanding than my father's neither her brothers, sisters, nor her father inspired us like my father's family. My grandfather (mother's father) "loved the sauce," even though he was the most successful of my great-great grandfather Jones' children. We never liked him in spite of his success because he was not as sociable as our grandfather. Therefore, Grandpa Coffers' (my father's father) place was the gathering place for us following church on the third Sunday of each month. We looked forward to this with eager anticipation, because he always had a game for us to play or a piece of candy.

My parents had five sons and because my twin died, my second brother and I are the oldest. My twin James Augustus died at five months. Oscar DePriest came one year later and now oversees the daily operations of the farm. The farm is still under cultivation and continues to grow cotton and peanuts as it always did. He is also a Deacon at our childhood church—the Quankey Baptist Church, in Quankey, North Carolina. Oscar is named for Oscar DePriest the son of slaves who became the first Black alderman and congressman elected from Chicago. My third brother Emmett Durant was named after another great Black figure, (my mother tried to name us all after great Black men). Emmett never married and was a lover of languages. He spoke about seven of them some of which were: Spanish, Algonquin, Chinese and Arabic. He spoke each language fluently. He lived in Washington, D.C., Puerto Rico and eventually moved to North Carolina where he died from kidney failure in August 2001. I tried my best to get him to go to medical school or get into research because he was such a good science student. His main interest was "love of the party." Winston Jerome is the one they called *red*. He is my mother's fourth son. He was so red that it looked as if blood was coming out of his cheeks when he was a child. When Winston was young, he quit school to work with our father. Daddy was cheap when it came to paying him. He kept almost everything that he made for himself and wouldn't equitably share in the wealth with the family

. After Winston was out of school for two years he left the farm and went back and finished his education He eventually married and now works in the Customer Service Department for the largest Honda Dealer in Maryland. He and his wife Atherene Richardson live in Silver Spring, Maryland. His wife is of Native American Heritage and grew up in a heavily populated Native American settlement known as the Saponi. They have two sons. John E. is a college graduate and works with the Bureau of Indian Affairs in North Carolina; their second son Daniel is also a college graduate and lives in Yonkers, New York. He is the Head of the Maintenance Department for a local hospital in the Bronx.

Lynn Thomas, the youngest, was a star athlete. He was the only brother who was born in the hospital which was in Roanoke Rapids. Lynn graduated from North Carolina Central College in Durham, with a B.S. Degree in Business Administration, but somehow the social life got to him. He decided to return to what he considered to be his roots and his Native American Group called the Saponi Nation. He returned to that habitat and lived like a hermit in a teepee. When he was found dead, we surmised that because of his love of animals, he probably tried to make friends with a water moccasin snake and was bitten to death. That was the way it looked. This tragic incident occurred around 1998 or 1999.

My daddy became a very successful farmer and businessman, and owned the largest grocery corner store in what was called the *Colored Town* of Roanoke Rapids, North Carolina. He also supplied acres of produce: Black eye peas, cabbage, collard greens and so forth to the farmer's market in Raleigh, North Carolina, our state capital and Roanoke Rapids as well.

I remember certain things as though they happened yesterday. Daddy was a neat freak and very finicky about his clothes and appearance, and aside from his proclivities he was a very intellectual man. He had a commitment to knowledge and read the local and statewide newspaper every day. Many people thought he was a school teacher but he only had a seventh grade education. In those days when you only had a seventh grade education people thought you were pretty advanced because most people didn't get further than the third grade.

In my opinion, Daddy was a perfectionist. One of the memorable things he did was to organize the community and improve the *bumpy* roads. He loved fine cars and didn't intend to drive his precious cars over bad roads. He was one of the largest farmers in that area and many of the people in our town worked for him. Working for him allowed them to send their children to school because they earned their living working on our family farm. Most townspeople worked for Daddy, and liked doing so because he was always fair. During the cotton picking season, he gave them a fish fry to close out the tobacco season.

Daddy was looked upon in his community as a history maker because I believe he bought his own farm of one hundred and twenty something acres when he was about twenty eight years old, when farming was *king*.

At that same time he bought one of the biggest grocery stores from his dear friend Joe Henry Branch. Mr. Branch was Black, and a very popular merchant and I worked as his cashier when I was in the third grade. That was an accomplishment for me because at the age of eight I was able to ring up sales and make change. Meanwhile, my parents worked together. My mother was sort of the bookkeeper and she kept all the names and telephone numbers of their workers on file. Many of the leading merchants who came out to our farm, looked up to Daddy because he was a man who never talked about what you couldn't do. Instead he talked about what you could do.

As a result of being a tobacco farmer, Daddy was a heavy cigarette smoker which he gave up in his fifties. However, he came down with emphysema which worsened and the disease took him at seventy-five. Mother remained a homemaker there on the farm and died at eighty-six. She continued to farm after Daddy died and was one of the first to be a produce farmer in the county. She didn't try to be a big a farmer like Daddy; instead she supplied the local farmer's market there in Roanoke Rapids. She also died as a result of tobacco poisoning which was from second hand smoke, plus she also dipped snuff. She died eight months after she was hospitalized. I made twenty-six trips home to see her and sat by her bedside until the end. We buried Mother with my father and brothers Emmett and Lynn in Enfield, in the cemetery across the street from the church, where I purchased twenty-five plots two years before my daddy died.

CHAPTER TWO

FARM LIFE

A Strange Move

Around five years old, I remember my parents purchasing their own farm in the Quankey community. This community was five miles from the nearest town in Roanoke Rapids, North Carolina and two miles off the main highway. It was recently named for my father because he was one of the most well-known and successful farmers in the area. To my knowledge Mother said that she was against naming roads, plants or flowers on one's property after he died. She felt that people should have enough pride in the deceased to name the roads after the landowners. Because Reverend Arthur Graham's lived on the front of Highway #48 and beside the path that goes back to our farm, she petitioned the County Commissioner to name the road "Graham-Scott Road." She got the neighbors to sign a petition, as well as some of the white farmers who farmed and did business with our father. I understand that there was a vote by the five member Board of County Commissioners and once it was passed, the orders were given to the Highway Department to put up the road sign.

I was very proud of our mother for being that proud of Daddy to name the road after him and to be so assertive, that she wanted something left as a monument in his honor.

Now moving to the Quankey community was our exodus away from our relatives and friends, which was a sad time for me. I was five, Oscar DePriest was four, Emmett Durant was three, Winston Jerome was one and Lynn Thomas was not yet born. I was sad because I was moving to *a strange land* where we didn't know anyone. I lost a great sense of belonging when I moved with my family. It was like starting all over again, as I was leaving my grandparents on my father's side as well as my cousins, schoolmates and playmates.

Growing up in the Quankey Community was very challenging because it was a new community that was unfamiliar. All of our cousins and relatives lived in Enfield and the Quankey community was thirty miles away from Grandpa Coffers and Grandma Olivia Scott. There were no paved highways except the famed Highway 301. The rest were dirt roads that were poorly kept and the travel hindered us from frequently visiting.

As a farmer Daddy was one of the most successful Black employers of field hands in the Quankey community. Most people called him Mr. Cofield. Daddy grew acres of peanuts, cotton and tobacco. Farmers worked together like a cooperative in cultivating and harvesting their crops. One man usually had the peanut picker that moved from farm to farm. They helped each other in harvesting the tobacco, although each man was on his own when he had to hire his own cotton pickers. Cotton was picked by hand. There were other farmers in the area, but Daddy remained the best known. He was the best known Black farm owner in the area for three reasons: 1—he owned over a hundred something acres of land; 2—he farmed for other farmers in addition to his own farms; and 3—he hired a lot of workers from town to work the farms.

As children we worked harder than the field hands. For one, we had to take care of all the cattle before 6:00 A.M. We rose each morning around 4:30 A.M. and worked from what was known as "From can't see to can't see." The stars would be out when we got up and came out in the evening time when the sun went down; so it was usually dark when we finished. In the cotton picking season, my brother Oscar and I had to make sure that all the cotton sheets were hauled to the barn by a mule and wagon, and dumped so that the workers had cotton sheets the following day.

During the tobacco season, we'd have to wrap the tobacco in bundles that were graded during the day by our parents. Sometimes we had to wrap the tobacco until late into the night. During land breaking, when we had a tractor, I broke land by the tractor's taillight so that I could go to school the next day. Breaking land was the term used for turning the soil over with a machine behind the tractor. The machine turned the soil about six inches deep, upside down, so that the soil would be soft for planting. After this, I usually ate, and when everyone was asleep, I completed my homework in the living room by the kerosene lamp. Kerosene lamps were the primary source of lighting then, as they were used before we had electricity in our home.

School Days

I attended a Rosenwald School. All of my schools were segregated schools—my Primary Grade, in the Daniels Chapel Community, and the First through Seventh Grades in the Quankey Elementary School in the Roanoke Rapids Township.

The Quankey Elementary School that I attended was located on Highway 48, which was a red clay unpaved highway. I attended Quankey beginning in the first grade through the second grade. My father, always a man of influence, convinced the Principal, Mr. D. P. Lewis of the John A. Chalomer High School to allow my brothers Oscar, Emmitt and me to attend the First and Third Grades respectively by riding on the school bus. We were hot shots to be going to the school in town when all the other kids from rural areas had to remain at the Quankey Elementary School. We rode the school bus and it was a great Third Grade experience. I formed lasting ties in the Third Grade that continue to this day. We were popular. Daddy had the largest corner store in town so it allowed my brother and I the chance to have our own money, when all the other kids didn't have any money. Imagine how shocked we were, when we were told at the end of the school year that we could no longer attend the school in town. The reason he gave was that the school bus was too overcrowded, so we were returned to the Quankey Elementary School. The news burst our bubble, and we immediately became the brunt of verbal abuse by one of the teachers. Of course, we couldn't say anything although we regretted not being allowed to ride the bus any longer. Nevertheless, we silently enjoyed feeling superior to the others kids, if just for a little while.

My second school was also a Rosenwald School, with of course all Black teachers and a Parent Teachers' Association (P.T.A.). The P.T.A. made powerful recommendations to the School Superindent as to whether teachers came or went at the end of the school year in the Quankey Community.

The Quankey School graduated students from the Fourth Grade to the higher grades. For the Fourth Grade's school closing ceremony, I recited a four page poem dedicated to Christopher Columbus. The poem *Rote*, was written as a play on words. I remained in the Quankey Elementary School until I graduated from the Seventh to attend the Eighth Grade at the John A. Chalomer High School, in Roanoke Rapids located in "Colored Town".

My father told me not to expect more than a Seventh Grade education. He actually said if we did that and made as much out of it as he had, then we would have done well! I became fearful that I would possibly not finish the eighth grade, so to impress my father I worked toward a straight A average in my eight grade year. I almost succeeded in earning mostly all A's and received two B's. From that time on my brother and I lived in *fear* that we were not only going to pass from one grade to the next, but that we would not graduate. Prayer became my morning vigil because on the farm we had about 10 chores to do before 6:00 A.M. During the farming seasons we had to make sure everything was in place, from shucking corn to feeding the mules, cows, chickens, as well as the hogs in a swamp located 500 feet away from the house. We also had to milk the cows, cut wood, make the fire and have fertilizer in the field. All this had to be done before we left for school. We would complete our chores at 7:00 A.M. run to the house, wash off, dress up and run two miles to meet the bus by 8:15 A.M. If we missed the bus, we had to return back to the farm to work.

I should note that in all the years we went to high school, we only missed the bus twice. The first time, someone who knew my father picked us up on the road which saved us the four mile walk to school. The second time when we heard our father's car, we hid in the woods until my father's car passed by. He evidently knew that we were too late to catch the bus. Therefore, he tried to play detective tracking us down to make sure we returned back to the field to work, but we outsmarted him.

In the eighth grade we had to choose an educational tract to follow— the Industrial Tract or the Academic Tract. Even though my father said he was not sending us to college, I chose the Academic Tract in spite of his comments. Some of my schoolmates were lamenting the words of their fathers–that they were not sending them to college either. However, as a fourteen year old youth, my mantra was, "I'd rather be prepared for a door that closed in my face, than have the door open and I not be ready to walk right in."

Ninth grade went well and I was hopeful that I could continue going to school at this same rate. Then in the 10th and 11th Grades, Oscar and I stayed out of school more than any other time. In the 11th Grade, we were out of school more than sixty-five days that year and sometimes two or three weeks at a time. My mother often broke down and almost cried, saying to our father, "To be sure Cofield, you're not going to let these children come this far and not finish, as they may need more education than you and I needed in our day." He fumed and fussed and eventually relented and we breathed a sigh of relief and ran off to school again.

In the meantime during this period, I went to Mr. Hudson, my homeroom teacher to ask a favor. I told him that I'd probably be out for several days and asked if I got my cousin to get the assignment from him, would he accept my homework. He said he'd think about it. So, determined to have it on his desk, I took my work to my cousin whose farm was next door to ours and was sure to give him a nickel each time.

Also in the ninth grade, I was chosen by *the New Farmers of America,* and was awarded a Jersey calf. The *New Farmers of America,* were the Black students who mastered the farming manual in the ninth grade. The white students of the segregated school were known as the *Future Farmers of America.* We competed with all the other schools in a state wide contest, because we were able to quote the New Farmers of America Manual verbatim. I came in second place in the State and was cited by Congressman L.H. Fountain of Tarboro, North Carolina.

I must say it was quite a leap of faith at such a young and tender age to choose the academic route, because I had no firm foundation on which to stand other than a flicker of hope. I never wavered in my goal to make it to college, like my uncles before me of whom my father was so proud. I remember that he talked about them all the time.

Daddy had six brothers and six sisters, and he was the third son of my grandparents on the Scott side. Abraham, the brother next to him, was looked upon as a prince in the family and the community. He was the first son of my grandfather and grandmother to attend North Carolina Central College, in Durham, North Carolina. Abraham was the first insurance agent in Halifax County to be employed by the largest Black insurance company—the North Carolina Mutual Life Insurance Company of Durham, North Carolina. Collin, my father's fifth brother, also graduated from North Carolina Central College and became a teacher.

Although my relatives lived in the Enfield farming community, also they visited us often in Roanoke Rapids, North Carolina. My parents' house was the gathering place for my uncles and aunts because my father was obviously the most successful and outstanding businessman farmer of his father's children.

Graduating High School with Honors

I was excited to enter the 12th grade, although there was no guarantee that I would be allowed to finish. This was farther than my father was allowed to go. His younger brother died from appendicitis when he was eleven. At the same time, Jasper and Frank, who were his two older brothers ran away and left all the farming on Daddy and my grandfather. Daddy dropped out of school to help his father run the farm, and because of this he didn't go any farther than the seventh Grade.

In the 12th grade, which was my senior year, I learned the speech of Toussaint L'Ouverture and the *Song of the Blind Plowman*. On the night of the recital it seemed as if my father didn't care whether I participated or not. He told me that I had to hill up some rows with the mule before I went anywhere. Then he drove off and left. I was crushed, whereupon my mother said, "John, go ahead and get dressed, I will hill the rows for you." I was ashamed that a woman, my mother, would handle the distributor. This was done with a two pronged blade in a circular fashion about twelve inches in diameter, pulled by a mule, with a space in the middle of the machine where the fertilizer came down in between the blades. The blades made a hill about a foot high, on top of which seeds were planted. The process was heavy and difficult to handle. Nevertheless, I went on my way with a weary heart, regretful that that was the only way I could make it to the senior play.

Much to my surprise, I graduated with honors. I graduated fifth in my class and wore the celebrated *honors* stole at the graduating ceremony. Also, I was one of only two students in my class who received scholarships to college. Virginia Union University gave me an $800 scholarship for four years, but nothing toward room and board. I felt proud of myself, yet didn't know what would become of me, or what I would do for the future. I knew that I couldn't return to the farm because Daddy wanted it all for himself, and didn't support education. So I had to make it on my own.

CHAPTER THREE

WORKING MY WAY
THROUGH COLLEGE

Resident of East Orange, New Jersey

During the week following graduation, Daddy asked me when I was going to leave. It broke my heart because growing up, he didn't allow us to go anywhere but to church and into the field to work. Now he asked me when I was going to leave when I didn't know anyone or have anywhere to go. Unknown to me, my mother wrote to her cousin Marie Brown in East Orange, New Jersey. She contacted her requesting to allow me to go live with her and her husband. My mother was so happy that she prematurely told Daddy before it was certain that I was going there. Thanks be unto God, Marie did send for me. I bought my own ticket and Daddy took me to the train station, put me on the train and said goodbye. I never felt so alone in all of my life, yet I had strong faith in GOD that *He was with me* and I would make it somehow.

Living in the city was shocking and grievous to me. I wasn't allowed to speak to my neighbors or holler across the street as I was use to back home where I grew up. I was accustomed to speaking to my neighbors and hollering at them in a friendly manner and they hollered back. Where I came from, this was how we greeted warm open hearted friendly people. This was all I knew.

Across the street from the house in which I was staying was the Calvary Baptist Church of East Orange, New Jersey. The pastor, Reverend William Bailey, instructed everyone not to hang out in front of his church. And after Sunday service, everyone was told to get in their respective cars and go home. This was amazing to me. It was the opposite of what I had known and grown up doing during my childhood. Church this way to me was *cold as ice*. I was used to a lively and warm fellowship service and after church let out I was used to meeting and greeting fellow parishioners with joy and gladness. I missed the Black Church experience of "call and response," because Calvary Baptist Church's congregation didn't respond verbally to the preacher during his sermon with a hearty "Amen," as was the custom in the South. Instead this church patterned its service after the white First Baptist Church across the street.

Evicted to the Y.M.C.A.

As my cousin (or surrogate mother) was fastidious about cleanliness, a requirement of hers was to remove my shoes before entering the house. Each day when she got home from work I was accused of doing something wrong. One day she just put me out and got a room for me at the Newark YMCA on Broad Street.

At eighteen years old I could have died from social isolation and loneliness because I didn't know anyone. I almost lost my mind and hungered for someone to know.

I couldn't sleep beyond 4:30 A.M. and many mornings, I stood at the window looking out onto the street to see if I saw anyone I knew.

I eventually met a Mr. Hankerson who worked at the "Y", and was also a friend of Marie. He was a pleasant man who always tried to break my Southern dialect and this made me very unappreciative of him.

Various Jobs in College

My first job was at Talchinsky's Pickle Works on Peshine Avenue in Newark, dumping bags of cucumbers into a four foot high barrel of brine. The floor was wet and sloppy and even if I wore an apron I got brine all over me, which made me "stink" like brine. Somehow I managed, because I knew that I wasn't going to be there for the rest of my life. I worked 58 hours a week, 7:00 A.M. to 7:00 P.M. weekdays and until noon on Saturday afternoon. I made $35.00 weekly and my rent was $15.00. I knew that I was being taken advantage of yet I was grateful for the job and eventually became the chemist on the second floor. In this position it was my responsibility to test the brine in the barrel to make sure that the barrel contained the right chemical strengths.

I soon left that job and got one as a janitor at an airplane parts plant in the Weston Electric Corporation on Frelinghuysen Avenue in Newark. Marie's brother Johnnie picked me up every afternoon. I worked second shift at night from 3:30 P.M. to midnight. He drove me to work and picked me up without ever getting a dime. I don't remember whether I offered him carfare or not because I was always in a bind for money. When Johnnie couldn't give me a lift, Marie's husband Smitty, frequently drove me to work on his way to his job which was about fifteen blocks away. Forty years later, in an effort to repay him for driving me to work, my brother Winston and I purchased a ticket for his lone lost daughter to travel from Seattle, Washington to Enfield, North Carolina to the annual family reunion.

Bloomfield College

In the Summer of 1956, my desire was to continue my education following high school, so I tried to save as much money as I could, although the job at Weston was not paying that much. I worked as a janitor, mopped floors, cleaned toilets and emptied garbage pails daily for a solid eight hours. I held onto my dream of going to college. The fall was getting closer so I decided to share my dream with Marie so that she would understand my leaving the Newark YMCA. Marie understood my desire to go to college and spoke to her pastor, Reverend Bailey, who personally knew Dean David Roberts, at Bloomfield College in Bloomfield, New Jersey. The door was open for me following their talk.

In the interim, that same summer, I left East Orange, New Jersey in 1956, and went home to North Carolina and sold my cow, ten pigs and the watermelon patch that I had grown since the 10th grade. I was still short $100.00 of the money I needed to enter Bloomfield College. I asked my father to lend me the remainder of the money but he refused. He said that he needed his money to buy himself a motor boat so that he could go fishing. His reply saddened me even though I knew that was the only pastime for farmers in the rural South. However, although my request was denied, I never gave up. The following day when I arrived from North Carolina, Marie asked me what my daddy said. After I told her, she said she had already decided to lend me the money.

So when I returned from home Marie told me to dress and she escorted me to Bloomfield College, and accompanied me to the Registrar's Office. While I waited for her outside the office, she came out, kissed me on the cheek and told me to go on to school. My dormitory room was in Siebert Hall, on the fourth floor corner. I was enrolled as a freshman and I was on my way. I was well received by the student body which was 99.9% white. There were only two other Blacks who entered with me, Al Conliff and Mary Jo Smith. Mary Jo, told me that the then President, Mr. Switzher said that she was the only Black he had admitted and that other Blacks who wanted to attend would only be allowed if she did well. I was outraged and said that he hadn't told me that and if he had I would have told him how wrong he was. I was not going to allow anyone to disrespect me like that regardless of who he was.

Since I was straight from the segregated South with all of its prejudices and hostilities, I internally harbored a great deal of resentment. I had no desire to get close to white folks and all of my classmates were white. I could never trust them as it was my "conception that" for the most part white folks couldn't be trusted.

One night, a fellow student, Bob Bergamester, who was a foreigner, asked me point blank why I didn't go along with him and the other students to the movies. I made the mistake of telling him that I didn't like Russians and Communist Chinese. He asked me if he told me that he was Russian would I refuse to ever speak or associate with him again. I was stunned by his question because I originally suspected he was Russian. Sure enough he was and in my book I already accepted him as a genuine person whom I admired and thought of a lot.

I was still working at night and attending classes during the day. I got in after 12:30 A.M. when I was used to going to bed no later than 9:00 P.M. and rising at 4:30 A.M. Now I got in after work, did my homework for an hour and tried to be in bed by 1:30 A.M. This schedule was numbing to my mind and body. In order to get some sleep and try to get up for breakfast at 7:00 A.M., I decided to forego breakfast which I never had done before. It was rough. The dietician, Mrs. Margaret Mead heard of my plight and began fixing me a lunch each evening to take to work. I still remember her name to this day— Mrs. Margaret Mead. I got out of class at 3:00 P.M. raced to my room to change my clothes, ran down through the kitchen, got my lunch and was across the street to catch the #120 Arlington Avenue bus at 3:15 P.M., in order to get to work on time.

I was working at Western Electric Corporation as a janitor. My job was to mop the plant toilets, scrub the latrines and empty all the garbage cans. I got hurt on the job during the first semester of my freshman year. After I reported to the plant infirmary, my injury was reported to the personnel office. It was concluded that I was *accident prone*. I did all I could do to keep my job. I was only eighteen years old and had no other source of support to keep me afloat or stay in Bloomfield College. My efforts were to no avail and I was released from the job in the dead of winter and continued to live on campus with no other source of income. What a loss for me. It was scary!

I took the Bloomfield Avenue bus to the end of the line in Newark after class each day looking for a job. During the ride, I stopped at each plant and begged for a job. After a week of trying, I was almost totally plunged into a state of depression. I didn't know what to do. At the various employment personnel offices I, visited I was constantly told that they were not hiring. Remember, I was only eighteen, skinny, weighed about 120 pounds and spoke with a southern drawl. I was frightened and scared to death to do something I had never done before. Up until that time I only worked on my father's farm. I was disappointed each time, but worked my way from factory to factory until 6:00 P.M. each evening. Most personnel offices were then closed. However, although I was sad, I ended each day with prayer. I got down on my knees and prayed to God for the next day. I always believed that God would answer my prayers.

I noticed a very kind upper classman who appeared considerate. I asked him if I could enter his room and tell him what was going on in my life. His name was John Kerry. He was encouraging and told me not to give up, but to go back and try one more time. I was so encouraged by his kind and gentle demeanor that hope came alive in me and I was inspired to go back and try again.

On the first day at the second stop which was the M.G.M. Record Company in Newark, I met the personnel manager. His name was Mr. George Staruch, and he hired me on the spot. He said that I should report to work on the following day. I was so glad to have a job that although I was wearing a white shirt, suit and tie, I begged him to go to work right then and there. However, he said, "My son, go home and change your clothes, because the job will be waiting here for you tomorrow." I went home, fell on my knees and thanked God for opening that door for me. I remembered my father's words growing up when he said: "When you leave home, you've made up your bed for the last time." It was either *root pig or die poor*. I was out on my own and had to make it the best way I could, so there was no point of asking for help.

I reported to work the next day following class. I worked the second shift from 3:30 P.M. until 12:30 A.M. My first job was to pick up scrap from the machine that produced the records, haul it to the back of this huge plant and dump it on top of a pile of scrap. The floor was very hard and I worked in dress shoes. My feet ached for almost two weeks before I became adjusted to the hard wooden floor. I did well on that job and moved up to a machine operator position where I wiped off the top of a hot iron plate that was as hot as fire. If the smooth surface of the iron plate wasn't wiped well, the record would sound pitchy and scratchy and popping could be heard in the record. There were no other Blacks who did that job and they surely didn't want a nineteen year old Black boy putting the finishing touches to Elvis Pressley records. After several attempts it was obvious that I was not cut out for that job and I was returned to hauling scraps. This was embarrassing because Black people told me not to try for the job. I went against their advice and I felt that I was a failure in their eyes.

I endured my circumstances until I moved from the production section to the inspection section as a *matrix expeditor* where there were only two of us in that department, Tommy Kinchlow the older white man and myself. I was warned by co-workers not go to that department because only whites wound up there. My foreman was Italian and he rode my back which seemed like almost every day. I took Frank Maffee's verbal abuse for almost a year until I saw a chance to become the only

Matrix Inspector on the night shift. I went around the foreman and approached a man named Fred Meyers, who was the Department Head. He was kindly disposed to me and gave me the highest paid job of any Black person in that department. I was twenty years old, when he told me to arrive to work wearing a white shirt and to look professional.

I worked at M.G.M .until my last semester of my senior year when both managers Fred Meyers and George Staruch approached me. They said that I worked too hard in order to put myself through college and I deserved some free time while I was still a student. They worked out a way that I could draw unemployment so that I could continue to have a source of income. I was overwhelmed. I heard it said by the preacher and in testimonies, "That God would not only make a way for you but he would rise up friends for you." I was elated and felt blessed, because both of them were like a father to me and because I felt close to them I invited them to my graduation and they came. Frank Maffee even apologized for the harsh treatment he dished out to me when I was under his supervision. I never looked back and told him that was in the past and that God was good to me and I was moving on. I later wrote a letter of thanks to both Fred Meyers and George Staruch respectively as I prepared to move on to seminary.

CHAPTER FOUR

CALL TO THE MINISTRY

Finding a Back Home Church

While I worked at Weston Instrument Corporation I felt the urge, *the pull* and the call to preach at eighteen years of age. I wrestled with that decision like Jacob wrestled with the Angel all night until he got the Angel to bless him. From then on I had no peace until I surrendered to *the call* to preach. I didn't want to disappoint my father because he lacked a high regard for preachers. He was a man who believed in *doing for yourself.* I went home to Roanoke Rapids that summer and told Daddy of my decision to preach to which he replied: "Well boy, you're getting ready to perish now." I hoped for his blessing, but it never came verbally.

I preached my first trial sermon in the summer of 1957 and was licensed to preach by the Reverend R. H. Kidd, the Pastor of the Quankey Baptist Church in Quankey. Quankey Baptist was full of folk singing, foot stomping, and hand clapping and *shouting* on feeling the spirit. It was a lively church and when the service was over, parishioners were glad to see each other on the church grounds. They ran to each other hollering from across the church yard as they passed each other at a distance. It was just a joyous time to get together with lots of smiles, laughter and mingling with visitors from neighboring churches who came to fellowship after church.

I had joined the Calvary Baptist Church in East Orange when I was a student at Bloomfield College. I attended the church with my cousin Marie Brown who was a member, along with her mother-in-law. Calvary consisted of an elite high class, Black congregation of which the Reverend William Bailey was the Pastor. He allowed me to sit in the pulpit sometimes, but most of the time I sat in the congregation. When I attended Calvary I worked with the Youth Fellowship which felt awkward because I was a youth myself. Reverend Bailey was a very warm and generous man and I will never forget that it was with his intervention that I was able to enroll at Bloomfield College. However, Calvary under his direction was very formal. They talked prayers and didn't *moan* them as I was accustomed to hearing. The service seemed quieter than a mouse. There were no "Amen's!" no chanting, no hallelujahs and the warm flowing spirit of the Quankay Church which I came out of was missing. It was just dead! For my own personal comfort, while I attended Bloomfield College in New Jersey, I continued to attend my down home country church. It met once monthly for Sunday service. All of the rural churches met once monthly, whereas Calvary held service every Sunday. It was during this period that some Blacks reached middle class status, owned their own homes, drove their own new cars and became pretty financially secure.

CHAPTER FIVE

CROZER THEOLOGICAL SEMINARY

Arrival at Crozer

In the fall of 1960, I packed my belongings into my brown and beige Rocket 88 Oldsmobile and headed to Crozer in Chester, Pennsylvania. I was off to Crozer never knowing that Rev. Dr. Martin Luther King, the Rev. Dr. Samuel Dewitt Proctor and other outstanding leaders were graduates of the seminary.

I ended up traveling in the opposite direction because I fell asleep at the steering wheel for the first time in my life. I was bewildered when I awoke and realized what occurred while I slept. It was the spirit that led me to travel farther south to the place where I belonged.

Crozer was like a dream come true. It reminded me of a reserved community in the Borough of Upland, Pennsylvania. I lived on the second floor of "Old Main", which was the school's dormitory and a former military hospital building used during the Civil War. On any given day, you could go to the top of the Belfry and look over the lawn and see the sunken graves on the school campus. There were no markers or headstones, and I wonder to this day if this fact was ever recorded.

On entering Crozer, I observed that the student body was friendly, and energetic about their academic pursuits. My entire class consisted of three Blacks, two white females and seven white males. I did not detect any prejudice among the students. They were all cordial and friendly.

The Student Bill Jones

The talk on campus was about a guy named Bill Jones. He was an upper classman and a senior who everyone was thrilled about. Everyone asked me if I met him yet. Then one day while walking along the cement walkway to Crozer's Becknell Library, I saw this tall towering *prince* of a person, and I immediately knew that he was Bill Jones. I approached him and asked, "Are you Bill Jones?" He replied, "I am, why do you ask?" I replied, "Everyone is talking about you and I'd like to be your friend." We became instant friends like David and Jonathan, the son of King Saul, a big brother to a little brother. It was similar to me being the oldest sibling in my family. He adopted me as his other brother on campus. He was married with a wife and son. Natalie was his wife's name. His son's name was Billy and he was two years old. He lived in the married students' quarters of a three story townhouse. After we became friends, Jones stopped by my room each morning before heading off to class.

The scare for the entire freshman class in seminary came from Dr. Jesse Brown, who was the professor of the Old Testament class. The results of his first test was that he only gave out two or three A's, a few B's and C's and D's for the rest of the grades. That struck fear in all of our hearts. I've never had too much difficulty learning, so I didn't panic like some of the rest of the students. We all read the first one hundred and sixty pages of James Finegan's *Light from the Ancient Past*. The assignment covered 3,000 years of Egyptian, Mesopotamian and Syrian History. I diagramed the reading onto two pages two days before the exam, memorized them, and was confident that I would earn one of the higher grades. Well after the exam, Dr. Brown wrote the grade on a piece of paper and then tore it off and dropped it into each student's mailbox. After the test, the fellows were sweating about their grades. I hid my grade because I knew some of the fellows studied for two weeks whereas I only studied for two days. When Bill Jones and all the classmates gathered in the lobby to inquire about the grades we received, Jones as I called him persuaded me to reveal my grade to the others as they did to each other. My grade was an A, to which one of the guys from West Virginia cursed. Jones replied, "Well, Harold some folks got it and other folks don't." This comment softened the anger towards me as most guys were aware of who studied and who didn't. When I made that A, it lessened my anxiety about failure, and I knew I was O.K. from then on.

Everybody rallied around Bill Jones, including our ethics professor, Dr. Kenneth Smith, author of *The Beloved Community* and a professor of Martin Luther King., Jr. Jones was very popular. Sometimes he led all of the students and some of the faculty to see the Philadelphia Warriors play when Julius Irving was the star player. The chapel in the seminary was always full whenever Jones preached. Attendance to chapel was not mandatory, but expected and we were all on the honors' system, even to not bring dates on campus.

Jones helped me with the first sermon I preached in the chapel at Crozer during the second semester of my freshman year. My first sermon was about the "Prodigal Son," and Jones gave me the outline. I was grateful for the help because it was mandatory that students preach one sermon per year.

Sometime during my sophomore year Jones was called to the Bethany Baptist Church in Brooklyn, New York. His leaving created a big void on Crozer's Campus, and school seemed dull after he left. Our relationship was very special and we remained close while he pastored at Bethany Baptist for forty-three years until his death in 2006.

I met the Reverend Dr. Harold A. Carter, in my freshman year. He was a recent Crozer graduate and the Pastor of the Court Street Baptist Church in Lynchburg, Virginia. We became close, and continue to remain dear friends. Jones once asked Carter to preach a Fall Revival at the First Baptist Church in Pascal, Pennsylvania where he was the Pastor at that time. I remember the sermon to this day which was on "The Holy Spirit," wherein he used the Hebrew and Greek terms, *ruach* and *pneumata*. I must say that this occasion was a great meeting for the three of us.

My First Car

When I arrived at Crozer I drove my 1955 Oldsmobile. The car was my first and the only possession I owned, so I needed to get a job to help maintain the car and support my education. I saved enough money to pay for enrollment and the first year of tuition. However, I was unable to find a job because the job market took a downward turn in 1960. Therefore, I was forced to *give up* my car because I could no longer afford the insurance, tires or the operating expense. Rather than let the car go to the dogs, I gave it to the son of the Campbell Family who were members of the Calvary Baptist Church in Chester, Pennsylvania where the late Dr. J. Pius Barbour was the Pastor. He was a Texas native and the first Black graduate of Crozer, who, by the way, made a proposition to the then President of the seminary. Dr. Barbour proposed that if he didn't make straight A's, the President could agree that no other Blacks would be allowed to attend Crozer Theological Seminary. Dr. Barbour not only made straight A's, but he went on to work on his Ph.D., at the University of Pennsylvania. I don't know if Dr. Barbour graduated from the University of Pennsylvania, but I do know that his dissertation is filed in the library at the University of Pennsylvania because I read it there.

I have good memories of Dr. Barbour. During my freshman year Jones took me down to Barbour's parlor, where Jones, and I debated the current theological issues of the day, church and denominational life. We did this on the local and national level. We often ended up in Barbour's dirty kitchen with dishes stacked up in the sink, where he washed off a saucer, took a pot, boiled some rice, and added some butter. We enjoyed our visits with Barbour eating his dirty rice. I graduated from Crozer in June, 1963. When I was called to be Pastor of the New Ahoskie Baptist Church in Ahoskie, North Carolina, Dr. Barbour, who was my seminary mentor convened an ordination council. The council included: Dr. Mel Henderson, New Testament Professor and Dr. Jesse Brown, Old Testament Professor both from Crozer Seminary; including Dr. Barbour. Following my ordination, I was officially installed as the pastor.

In retrospect, I am so deeply indebted to him because I had no money when I entered my senior year, My mother asked me not to go back for fear I would lose my mind. I replied, "Yes, mother, I will lose my mind If I don't go back to Crozer. I have to go back." I attended Crozer for the three required years. However, when I registered for my senior year in 1963, Dr. Jesse Casterlowe, the Vice President asked me how much tuition I was paying for the semester. I replied: "$15.00". Then he stated that he required a better report for President Dr. Sankey Blanton. So he asked me, "Do you have a job?" In faith I said, "Yes." He asked, "How much are you making?" I thought right quick and said $50.00 to which he asked, "Then will you pay $10.00 a week?" I said, "Yes." I gave him my last $15.00, went to my bedroom, fell down on my knees and prayed on my behalf. Before I finished praying to God, I received a call from Dr. Barbour. He said, "Scott, why don't you come on down here and work for me. I will give you $50.00 a week" (This would be the equivalent of nearly $500.00 or more today). I came to love him as a dear grandfather figure.

During my second year at Crozer, I followed Bill Jones as the Interim Pastor of the First Baptist Church at Pascal, in Pennsylvania. While Jones was at Pascal, he was called to pastor the great historic Bethany Baptist Church in Brooklyn, New York. His former church voted to accept his recommendation that I would be the *Supply Pastor*, until the church elected a full time Pastor. I was privileged to attend his installation as Pastor at which his father the Reverend William A Jones, Sr., preached. Jones' father was Pastor of the Pleasant Green Baptist Church in Lexington, Kentucky, which was the oldest Black baptist church west of the Mississippi. Jones' family consists of a long succession of ministers: his grandfather was a minister and two of his brothers are ministers.

Sometime in my last year at Crozer, I noticed an offer posted on the school's bulletin board for scholarship grants. Students qualified if they wrote a fifteen page essay and mailed it to the Rockefeller Doctoral Fellowship Foundation in Princeton, New Jersey. I followed the Instructions and to my great joy I received a scholarship. It paid the remaining balance of my junior year and all of my senior year. "Glory be to God." I graduated debt free!

Also at the beginning of my final year at Crozer, the National Sunday School and the National Baptist Congress met in St. Louis, Missouri. Jones was already a pastor and he, together with another pastor, asked me to join them in driving to St. Louis. As usual, I didn't have any money and only had but $5.00. Jones told me if I could take care of my food I didn't have to worry about a place to stay as I would stay with them. I never dreamed that on our first night in St. Louis, we would dine with Dr. Martin Luther King and his guests. They all ate steak and when they came to me, I said, "Hamburger, please." I figured the $5.00 would last me a week if I ate one hamburger with a milk shake each day. However, Jones overrode me and said, "Give him a steak too." I was in heaven.

Many memorable things happened while I was a seminary student at Crozer, such as meeting several luminary ministers during my years of study there.

One day as I worked in the kitchen pulling the dumbwaiter to the first floor dining room, Dr. Samuel Proctor walked in. I was overjoyed to come face to face with him. As Black men, we were joyful and delighted that alumnus Dr. Samuel Dewitt Proctor, became the head of the Peace Corps in Nigeria, and was named to Crozer's Board of Directors while we were still students. To see him on our campus along with the other Board Members was like looking at "Christ come to earth." Proctor was an inspiring figure. I never dreamed that we would pastor together in Harlem—he at the Abyssinian Baptist Church on 138th Street while I was at St. John's the Baptist on 152nd Street. I was invited to do retreats and services for him at Abyssinian, but my schedule always conflicted. I am grateful that he was the installation banquet speaker for me when I became pastor of St. John's in 1972.

During my third and final year at the seminary, while attending the National Baptist Congress in St. Louis, I met the popular Reverend Dr. Moses Newsome. Rev. Newsome was the pastor of the historic First Baptist Church in Charleston, West Virginia. He was also professor of philosophy at West Virginia State in Charleston, West Virginia. He discovered that I was from his nearby home of Ahoskie, and said if I ever needed him to let him know. When I returned to Crozer in Pennsylvania, I wrote Dr. Newsome with questions about his home church in Ahoskie. His response was to schedule me to preach there on the first Sunday before Christmas in 1962, during the first semester of my last year.

On the first Sunday in January of this same year, I was called to pastor but began my pastorate duties on the fourth Sunday. I commuted by train from Chester, Pennsylvania and returned back to school that following Monday evening. Many of the students worked in local churches on Sunday. Therefore, Crozer didn't have classes on Monday. Instead weekly classes were scheduled on Tuesday of each week.

There was an occasion when I attended a freedom rally at the Bright Hope Baptist Church of Philadelphia. The church was pastored by the Reverend Dr. William Gray, Sr.—the father of Bill Gray, Jr., former Congressman and former Director of the United Negro College Fund. The rally was held by the Baptist Minister's Conference of Philadelphia, where Dr. King was the keynote speaker and I had the privilege of formally meeting him.

Although I previously met Dr. King, I was hearing him speak to an audience for the first time. The Bright Hope Baptist Church, in Philadelphia, Pennsylvania seated about 1200 parishioners and it was filled. I accompanied Bill Jones to the rally, along with other ministers. Dr. King's speech was very moving and it made a lasting impression on me. I was curious about the philosophy of nonviolent direct action which was his philosophy. I listened attentively as Dr. King explained his strategy of *nonviolence* and as he said, "If they strike you on the check, still love them, if they spit on you, still love them." I was stunned to hear him say that, because I believed in self defense at that time. I felt honored to shake his hand at the conclusion of the program, and found him to be very gracious. He made me feel like I belonged in his group and encouraged me to continue to do good work at Crozer, his alma mater.

I was familiar with his leading the Montgomery Bus Boycott that outlawed discrimination in interstate travel. I knew this because I frequently traveled back and forth by train from Newark, New Jersey when I was a student at Bloomfield College, and from Philadelphia to Crozer, Pennsylvania when I was a student at Crozer. I was aware of Blacks having to switch cars and move to the back of the train when arriving at the Union Street Station in Washington, D.C. This was very humiliating. So when the law passed that outlawed discrimination in interstate travel, there was a deep sigh of relief that Blacks didn't have to travel at the back of the trains in the south anymore, or switch cars on arriving in Washington, D.C. since Washington was below the Mason Dixon Line.

Meanwhile, I returned to campus fired up. I saw on television that Black people were hiding in bathtubs in Alabama to keep from being shot and/or killed by the Ku Klux Klan as they rode through Black communities shooting into Black people's houses. I blew up in Dr. "Snuffy" Smith's class.

The following morning in class, I told Dr. Smith that he could take his lectures back because it was all theoretical and didn't apply to the situation in which my people found themselves. I told him and the class that we (Blacks) weren't taking it anymore and that we were going to bring a stop to such brutality. Since my attack was professional Dr. Smith, professor of Christian ethics was not insulted. He said, "Scott, we understand how you feel, but take it easy." Well when he said, "Take it easy," I said, "That's the problem, we've been taking it easy too long and we ain't taking it anymore." The class was in a hush and the students seemed to respect how I felt. As I sat in the front row, I was surprised that Dr. Smith didn't throw me out of the class or even suspend me. Anyway, I knew from then on that I was highly visible, and someone to be watched.

In the second week of February, 1963 the Better Citizen's Club of Hertford County, an organization of all Black males, invited the Reverend Dr. Wyatt Tee Walker to be their keynote speaker. Rev. Walker was the Executive Secretary for Dr. King's S.C.L.C. I was so inspired that the rally was covered in the *Hertford County Herald Newspaper,* that I bravely took the article back to Crozer and posted it on the bulletin board without permission from the President or the Dean.

When Dr. Smith saw the article, even though I had been in Ahoskie as a pastor for only two months, he told me not to go too fast. Well, whether I went fast or not, segregation should never have existed in the first place. I felt that I was supposed to do everything I could do to end such cruelty to Black people.

Sometime in 1965, I was greatly surprised that Dr. King was scheduled to be the Centennial Celebration speaker at my first church. He was unable to attend and instead sent Reverend Dr. Marshal Shepherd, Sr., Pastor of the Mt. Olivet Baptist Church of Philadelphia and the most powerful preacher in Philadelphia. I never dreamed that later Rev. Shepherd would be on the S.C.L.C. Board that hired me to be the Executive Secretary of Operation Breadbasket of Greater New York and Vicinity.

The Call to Pastor

After landing my first church I was ready to follow in Dr. King's footsteps.

When I received *the Call* to pastor, at the new Ahoskie Baptist Church, in Ahoskie, North Carolina, I sat down and wrote a letter to

God the contents of which said, "I do not know what path I will follow, but I do pray that whichever path I take, You will be with me."

The Call to New Ahoskie Baptist Church was where I was elected to be the pastor of a well-known church. I felt that my prayer to be called to pastor a church had been answered and I felt blessed above and beyond the ordinary to be elected pastor of a church in the town that was so well known for progressive Blacks, landowners and business operators. To be only fifty miles from where I grew up was more than I could ask. I was promised a decent salary which was sufficient income. Now I didn't feel left out anymore. Rev. Jones and Rev. Harold Carter had their own pastorate. I now had mine and we were equal.

It was 1963, I was graduated from Crozer, and now took my journey by train from Chester, Pennsylvania to Ahoskie, North Carolina to become the full-time pastor with a salary offer of $87.50 per week: no insurance, no pension or retirement plan, just a flat salary of $87.50 per week, and I was grateful.

Dr. Newsome, who was also the president of the West Virginia Sunday School Congress, scheduled me to preach for the Congress that met in Bluefield, West Virginia, and on Sunday at his church. This historic First Baptist Church was previously pastored by two nationally known ministers: the Rev. Dr. Vernon Johns, predecessor to Dr. King, at the Dexter Avenue Baptist Church in Montgomery, Alabama and the late Dr. Mordecai Johnson, the former president of Howard University.

I met Dr. Vernon Johns at the Calvary Baptist Church when Dr. Barbour asked him to bring greetings at the close of a Sunday afternoon service. During his salutation, Dr. Johns lifted up the life of "John Brown" and stated that he was at Yale sometime back and asked some of the white students there if they knew John Brown. They replied that they didn't know him and they didn't give a damn. The congregation was shocked and Dr. Johns proceeded to tell them that they needed to subscribe to his *Twentieth Century Magazine.* The congregation became restless to which Dr. Johns replied, "I see they didn't give a damn, and you don't give a damn either," and sat down. Prior to then, I had heard various stories about Dr. Johns but after that one chance meeting, I never forgot him.

Following the Sunday sermon at Dr. Newsome's church, we proceeded to travel by car to the National Congress of the National Baptist Convention, Inc., meeting in Birmingham, Alabama. When we arrived, we lodged at the A.G. Gatson Motel, owned and operated by the late A. G. Gatson, who was the treasurer of the African Methodist Episcopal (A.M.E.) Church. Gaston was a successful entrepreneur who also owned the Booker T. Washington Bank that was located across the street from the motel.

The Birmingham Movement

The Birmingham Movement was just ending. Some of the debris was still smoldering and the streets and tensions were high. On Tuesday night of the convention, Dr. Ralph Abernathy promoted Dr. King's latest book. The book, *Strength to Love*, was just released and Dr. Abernathy sold it during an evening session. On this same evening, Dr. Johnson spoke on the global situation facing people of color around the world. I remember that I first heard Dr. Mordecai Johnson speak at the Orange High School in Orange, New Jersey when I was eighteen years old. He was a captivating speaker, and had the ability to recite statistics like Jesse Jackson, and I was impressed with his grasp of history and statistics.

Traveling to Birmingham was not a glowing time because of the violence, terror and brutality that terrorized Black people all over the country. Like most Black parents, my parents were not too excited about me being involved. Parents were cautious and fearful for the lives of their children. There were no words of congratulations or praise. Whatever happened, you mostly kept it to yourself, as many parents felt that we were breaking the law and disrupting the peace. Anyway, following the convention, Dr. Newsome and I motored to his home town of Ahoskie and I went home to Roanoke Rapids which was about thirty-five miles away.

My arrival home was a joyous and momentous occasion. Mother was always happy to see me, both of my younger brothers, Winston and Lynn were ecstatic and Daddy was casual as usual. He never seemed excited about anything I did or anyone of us did, for that matter.

CHAPTER SIX

MY FIRST CHURCH

First Civil Rights Speech

From the beginning of my arrival in Ahoskie as pastor of the New Ahoskie Church, *freedom rallies* were held monthly. This was done to update and keep the community informed and in touch with what was happening in the neighboring counties, in the state and around the nation. These monthly meetings began under a local Black leadership group–The Better Citizens of Hertford County, North Carolina under the direction of Raymond Grant, who was a member of my church and the second Black on the Ahoskie Police Force.

Charles McLain the guest speaker for the evening was completely overcome by the killing of the four little girls at the Sixteenth Street Baptist Church in Birmingham. Therefore, when it came time for him to speak, he wasn't able to do so and he literally slumped down into his chair following the introduction to speak and openly wept. A hush came over the rally and the feelings that were just so high plunged into despair and it was as if the Lord laid His hands on me and said, "Now you have to speak, stand and I will put words in your mouth." I rose and faced the audience, and was told by the Spirit, "Just tell them, what you've been through, and that you're not going to take it anymore." I never gave a public speech before, but I knew that we couldn't end the rally on a *down note.* So for the first time in my life, and at the age of twenty-five, I stood up and began to speak and said,

> "Brothers and Sisters, I'm tired of being told I have to go to the back of the bus. I'm tired of riding the back of the bus, or the back of the train to Washington, D.C., coming from Bloomfield, New Jersey. I'm tired of being put out of restaurants when I want to eat like anybody else. I'm tired of being told I can't sleep in hotels because of my color. I'm tired of our mothers being treated like girls and our fathers like boys. I'm tired of our race being treated as we have been across the years. We aren't going to take it anymore. We're going to march, rally and protest, until the walls of segregation come tumbling down."

It was about a five-minute speech, and then I led them in singing our closing song, "We Shall Overcome." To my surprise, the audience was ecstatic. I was surprised at myself because I never took a *leap of faith* like that before in my life. I never before spoke publicly to an audience at a freedom rally. I remember Mrs. Dora Newsome, who was a school teacher and parishioner of New Ahoskie Church not being afraid when she approached me and said, "Reverend, you had us so fired up, all you had to say was let's march, and I would be the first one in the line." I knew that I made a hit in my speech,—the gauntlet was launched and there was no turning back for me. I had plunged head long hands and feet, into the midst of the Civil Rights Struggle. I also saw that the people were with me and all eyes were upon me, especially white people of the city and the Ku Klux Klan, in particular. I had cast my lot and my life to die for the cause of freedom and justice for our people. My prayer from then on, was "Lord, be with me." I felt His Spirit and I felt that I was doing what God wanted me to do in ending the violence against my people who meant no harm to anyone—who wanted to be treated right and with respect, like anyone else.

The First Community College

After I became established in Ahoskie, I continued to be involved in what the movement called Freedom Rallies. On the third Sunday afternoon in July, 1964 I invited Mr. Charles McLain, the field secretary of the North Carolina Branch of the N.A.A.C.P, to be the speaker. This was the same Sunday that the Sixteenth Street Baptist Church was bombed in Birmingham, Alabama, and where the four little girls were killed as they attended Sunday School.

After the rally that followed, Mr. McLain shared with the N.A.A.C.P officers the opportunity to introduce a community college for locally displaced farmers, and suggested that we should meet with a Mr. Jernigan, the then House of Representative Leader, to ask him to introduce a bill to establish a community college in Hertford County. This was during election year and there was a very popular radio announcer from Murfreesboro, North Carolina running as a candidate for the same office. Members of the executive committee, Carlos Brown, Vice President, George Hall, 2nd Vice President, Augustus (Gus) Chavis, Treasurer and Reverend James A. Felton, Secretary met secretly with Mr. Jernigan and he pledged to introduce this bill for a community college, if the N.A.A.C.P members would throw their support behind him. We made the difference in his success and he kept his word. He saw that the first community college was established in the Choanoke area; although it was opened in Bertie County.

Today, there are now community colleges in every eastern Carolina County, including my own home County of Halifax County. The names of Carlos Brown, Gus Chavis, George Hall and John L. Scott should be engraved on the cornerstone of Hertford Community College as the founders, as a result of a secret meeting. We were the men who persuaded Representative Jernigan to introduce the legislation to the City Fathers.

City Council Meetings Begin

I then proceeded to attend the town council meetings of Ahoskie that week, to which no Blacks ever attended. At the time passing legislation banning rallies and marches in the streets of Ahoskie was being considered. I was a person taken over by the spirit of prophecy. I pleaded with the City Fathers not to pass such legislation, but to form *good neighbor councils* in order to end the laws of segregation in our town. My argument was joined by Joseph I. Parker, Sr., who was the owner and publisher of the Hertford County Herald Newspaper, and he implored the city council to take a more constructive course. Our voices were not heeded and the legislation was passed. I was possessed by the spirit and quoted the words of Ezekiel, "You have sown to the wind and you shall reap the whirlwind." After that I left, only to have the Pastor–Rev. L.E. Terrell of the (white) First Baptist Church of Ahoskie at my door the next day, welcoming me to the town asking me to be more tolerant toward the ordinance that just passed. He was a gracious person but I knew he didn't come there to help us in our struggle, but to appease me. I was saddened by his gesture and knew he came not to speak the voice of God but the voice of the powers that were in his church.

Williamston's North Carolina Police Chief

Just around this time, I attended an interracial clergy council meeting that was organized by a young Episcopal priest by the name of Kimsey King. He was twenty-seven and concerned. He was alarmed that the Mayor, Charles I. Pierce and City Manager McIntosch, in his opinion were considering bringing the worst police chief in Martin County from Williamston, North Carolina to Ahoskie to keep us in place.

This chief at Williamston was known for using *cow prods* against the demonstrators there. Along with that practice, while riding horses, he and his police chased the T.J. Hayes High School students down the hallway on horseback and onto the grounds of the campus. It was so bad that the North Carolina Teachers' Association, headed by a Mr. Lyons, drafted a petition to the Governor of North Carolina to prevent the police from continuing this practice. When I heard this I took off for Williamston with my recorder in my pocket to gather evidence to prevent the Chief of Police from Williamston from coming to Ahoskie. Reverend C.A. Hart, Elder Statesman of Hertford County and a pastor of several strong country churches, heard that I was going and joined me on the trip. We obtained the petition written by the North Carolina Teachers' Association and recorded the voice of a Mr. Styron Barnes, the merchant who operated his store next door to T. J. Hayes High School. Reverend Hart and I then summoned a meeting with Mayor Pierce and Mr. McIntosch, City Manager of Ahoskie and presented our findings. We were informed that the contract was already signed and we were asked for our support. I replied, "If a police chief dragged your mother out of her church down the steps and she was four months pregnant, could you support such a person?" They saw, by whatever means, we were determined to protect our town by not allowing that chief to come, and we concluded the meeting by informing them that a meeting would be held at New Ahoskie Church that would fight to deal with that situation.

After we left I received a call that same day from a leading Black undertaker, asking me to come to his office for a meeting. I thought it might be a meeting to offer other options, but it was not. The purpose of the meeting was for me to call off the meeting at New Ahoskie Church and let the Good Neighbor Council handle it. After debating the meeting for an hour, I saw that further discussion was futile, whereupon the other gentleman, who was a member of my church, stuck out his foot, to block my exit and said, "You ain't going nowhere." I didn't know what to expect—whether I was going to be attacked or not. I just didn't know. So, as scared as I was, I first sat down, took a deep breath, and eventually my nerve came back. Then I just walked out.

The meeting was held that night at 7:30 P.M. Reverend Hart and I presented our findings, and those present voted unanimously that all effort should be taken to prevent the chief from coming. We never got an official word, but thank God, our efforts prevented the Williamston chief from coming to Ahoskie. We got it through the grapevine that the contract was cancelled and calm prevailed.

Deplorable High School Supplies

It came to my attention that the school situation for students at the all-Black R. L. Vann High School was deplorable. The rooms had no closets to hang up coats, the desks lacked bottoms to store books, and the science laboratory was appalling and deficient. I was driven *by the spirit* to inform the principal of the protests who came to us and that we the N.A.A.C.P was asked to intervene in gathering the facts. Mr. Cooper, the principal, said, "Brother, Pastor, do what you must do, I will not stand in the way." Mind you, this was 1963, almost ten years after the 1954 Brown vs. The Board of Education decision. I gathered the facts and had Joe Parker, Manager, of the Hertford County Herald, to print the data in the local newspaper. Nothing changed, whereupon Carlos Brown of the N.A.A.C.P and I went to see Mr. R. P. Martin, the Superintendent of Hertford County Schools, and told him that the Supreme Court outlawed segregation in public schools and asked was he going to enforce it? He said, "No." We informed him that it was the law of the land, but he intended to do nothing. We attempted to bring the two Black schools together—the Robert L. Vann School of Ahoskie and the Riverview School of Murfreesboro with the consent of both the principals. Mr. Boe, the principal of Riverview High School was incensed that anyone would try to do anything about the school situation in Hertford County. The meeting took place over his protest regarding the role the schools should play regarding segregation. I had to file a federal suit against the Hertford County School Board in order to bring about the integration of the school system. In the meantime, the March on Washington was building momentum all over the area, and our attention turned to that direction.

Attempt to Integrate the Tommy Hawk Restaurant

In the meantime, I received a call from John Woodley from the neighboring town of Murfreesboro. He was a white minister and a recent graduate of Wake Forest Seminary in North Carolina. He asked me to join him in integrating the Tommy Hawk which was the most popular restaurant in Ahoskie. I was filled with trepidation and the thought that I couldn't have this white boy dare me to do something that I hadn't yet done. Nevertheless, we went together to the Tommy Hawk and sat down. We waited for a waiter to come to our table but none ever came. Finally, Mr. Bracey, the manager came over and said, "We don't serve colored and white together in our restaurant", to which

John replied, "We don't see it on the menu, all we want is some food." Bracey then bristled up but said, "We're not integrated, get out before I call the police and have you thrown out because you are white." I said to John. "Let's go." I not only feared for my life, I feared for him more than myself. He was from the neighboring town of Murfreesboro which was only ten miles away, and where his mother was the well-known town librarian. We left and promised to meet again to go to the movies or something.

The next day, while I sat in my office, I received a call from the restaurant owner Bracey, saying he was sorry for what he did. He was not aware that I was the Pastor of New Ahoskie Baptist Church and that I was welcome to come back at any time. He wanted me to call him in advance so the way would be okay, because he just didn't want any rank and file Blacks coming into his restaurant. I told him that I saw white men in overalls, brogan shoes, and grease monkeys and wasn't returning because I had already been there. I wasn't going back until Blacks could go to his restaurant like everyone else, because when I left Ahoskie, I faced the same plight like any other "colored person."

Ed Weeks and I Denied Restaurant Service

I was previously refused restaurant service in Wilmington, Delaware, while I was still at Crozer. It was following the election when Ed Weeks, a white student and an upper classmate and I were elected by Crozer's Student Body to represent Crozer at the Seminarian Conference in Wake Forest, North Carolina. That night Ed and I stopped at this restaurant. We went in and he was in front of me as we stood in line. When the server got to Ed, he refused to serve him because I was with him. In order to eat, I had to wait in the car while Ed got food for both of us. Seriously speaking, the Seminarian Conference was a great get-together with students coming from Canada. The late Carlyle Marney, who was a white Southern Baptist Pastor, of Myers Baptist Church in Charlotte, North Carolina, and the founder of Interpreters House, Black Mountain, North Carolina was the speaker. He was a breath of fresh air. The following year the next Seminarian Conference was held at Crozer, and I was the coordinator. Reverend Dr. Wyatt Tee Walker, was the guest speaker, along with Dr. John Skoogland, New Testament Professor at Colgate Divinity School, in Rochester, New York.

The March on Washington

One July morning, Bill Jones called me and reminded me of the upcoming "March on Washington." Prior to Jones' call, I really hadn't decided to attend. The press said that violence would characterize the rally and for fear of my life I didn't want the Ku Klux Klan to know that I would attend the march. However, when Jones called, it was just the motivation I needed. Due to our distant locations of Brooklyn, New York, we agreed to meet at the Union Street Train Station in D.C., at 8:00 A.M. I left in the dark of night, so that the police who were watching me wouldn't notice me leaving. Jones and I met as agreed and walked with the throngs of people to the great lawn of the Lincoln Memorial. It was a hot day. President John F. Kennedy tried to persuade A. Philip Randolph to call off the marchers who came to D.C. by bus or train. The flow of people never stopped. They disembarked singing, "Woke up this morning with my mind set on freedom," and "Don't ya let nobody turn you around, keep on walking keep on talking, walking up to freedom land."

The atmosphere was *lit up* with freedom songs, banners and placards representing every labor organization, church, fraternity, sorority and other groups. Gospel singer Mahalia Jackson opened the rally singing, "Soon One Morning." Among the speakers were Reverend Adam Clayton Powell, John Lewis of S.N.C.C, James Farmer of C.O.R.E., Roy Wilkins of the N.A.A.C.P. and Whitney M. Young of the National Urban League.

Everyone waited for Dr. King. When he arrived, A. Philip Randolph introduced him as the "Conscience of the Nation," and the crowd went wild. Dr. King was at his best and gave the "I Have a Dream" speech and closed on the famous words, "Free at Last, Free at Last, Thank God A 'mighty, I'm Free at Last!"

The march ended around 4:00 P.M. and the crowd dispersed. On my way back home I hoped that it wouldn't take long for the pending Civil Rights Bill to be signed by John F. Kennedy, even though he initially tried to get A. Philip Randolph and others to call off the march.

Jones and I parted, he traveled North back to Brooklyn, and I on to Ahoskie with *Dreams* of a better day and a better America, where Black and white could get along with each other by tearing down the walls of hostility. I knew we had a lot of work to do and there was a long road ahead of us, because the Civil Rights Bill still had to be signed by President Kennedy.

John Kennedy's Assassination

Then President John Kennedy was assassinated, and our dreams of a better America were dashed. When Kennedy was assassinated, Lyndon Baines Johnson came to the forefront of freedom in ways we never dreamed. That he was a Texan, made us doubtful. However, when he signed the Civil Rights Bill of 1964, it was similar to Abraham Lincoln, signing the first Emancipation Proclamation of 1863. We knew that our work was cut out for us and that we had to *rush* while the door of opportunity was slightly cracked open.

We were mindful of the short window of opportunity that we Blacks had experienced between 1865 and 1879, before President Andrew Jackson took the troops out of the South and turned Black people over to the Ku Klux Klan to be hung, whipped and slaughtered by them. Furthermore we were certain that President Lyndon Johnson wouldn't be re-elected for having signed the Civil Rights Bill in 1964. So we figured that the time to act, to keep rallies, marches and protests would completely bring down the walls of segregation in schools, restaurants, hotels and places of employment.

Hazen Foundation Honors

In The Summer of 1965, I was invited by the Hazen Foundation to study "The Negro in the Christian Ministry", for an upcoming conference. The Hazen Foundation is a private foundation that was founded in 1925 and is committed to supporting the leadership of underprivileged children and young people. The conference was held on the campus of Virginia Union University in the month of July.

I was one of forty chosen for this conference. It was quite an honor, because I was only twenty-six going on twenty-seven years old. I didn't share the news with my congregation because the opinion of the officers was that I might get "A Big Head" since we had successfully gotten Blacks hired for the first time in the Ahoskie Bank and the Telephone Company. I traveled to Richmond, Virginia, the Virginia Union University and Seminary Campus, and stayed on the campus until departure time on Fridays at 4:00 P.M.

The late Rev. Dr. Y. B. Williams, Pastor of the Historic First African Baptist Church, in Richmond Virginia became a close confidential friend, along with his new wife, Gracie, who was somewhat younger than he. I also made a lifetime connection with Dr. Carlyle Marney, the keynote speaker, lecturer for the conference. Aside from being a Pastor, he was a nationally known author who had just published his latest book *Beggars in Velvet. The* experience was both challenging theologically and rewarding spiritually.

Back in Ahoskie, we continued to have our monthly "Freedom Rallies" sponsored by the Hertford County's N.A.A.C.P. Political Action Committee. With the passage of The Civil Rights Bill of 1964, we were determined to integrate everything possible from top to bottom. I had a group to meet at New Ahoskie Church. Together with the N.A.A.C.P, to test the law going into effect, we gave young people money to go to the lunch counters, restaurants, the movie theaters and the 5 and 10 cent stores to determine if the passing of the Bill was working in our favor.

Bank Begins to Hire Blacks

In 1964 I served notice on the Ahoski Bank as well as the telephone company, that if they did not hire at least one Black by a certain Friday evening, we would continue demonstrations until someone was hired. By Friday of that week, the Ahoskie Bank hired its first Black employee. She was Mattie Watford, the former secretary of the Black-owned and operated Tri-County Credit Union. The Telephone Company hired Janice Pierce as the first Black telephone operator. We demanded the same of the largest drive-in eatery. We held a rally on the Saturday that was attended by Grandmother Olivia Scott, and my other grandmother, Pearlie Jones and Uncle Percy Scott, my father's brother.

At the rally, I asked, "How many colored folk do we have working at the Tasty Freeze?" I replied, "Not nary a one." The paper reported that I said, "Not a damn one." And I was furious. It was an unthinkable word to be spoken in a Black church from the pulpit at that time, especially since my grandmothers and uncle were sitting in the audience. Even though the rally was recorded, the reporter refused to retract his statement. You weren't supposed to dispute white folks. As a Black man you could never be right if a white man said you were wrong. Anyway, persons were eventually hired at the Tasty Freeze. The trick was to favor whites by hiring a colored person who you could not tell was white or Black.

Therefore, we had to reprimand the City Fathers from practicing such a nefarious policy of hiring *light-skinned* Blacks over dark-skinned Blacks. Immediately after this, Carlos Brown from Winston, North Carolina and I led an N.A.A.C.P. membership campaign in 1964 in order to boost our membership. We did this so that if we were ever arrested and needed the N.A.A.C.P. Legal Defense Fund, we'd have the nationally known organization to defend us.

First Black for County Commissioner and the Board of Education

With such a tremendous increase in enrollment, we considered organizing a Political Action Committee (P.A.C.) of Hertford County for the purpose of electing Blacks to the Hertford County Board of Education and the County Commissioner's seat.

We called a meeting at what was known as the "Ambassador's Club," a private social club operated by the Black social elite. Many of them belonged to the New Ahoskie Baptist Church where I pastored. The response from all over the county was good, and at that time in 1964, we pledged to contribute $50.00 each in order to underwrite the candidates' campaign. We also approached Mr. Howard Hunter, a very popular undertaker for candidacy of the Board of Education and the well known pastor, Reverend Chester A. Hart of Ahoskie for

County Commissioner. The money came in good and we were on our way.

Floyd McKissick Rejected

To spark a good voter turnout, we (The N.A.A.C.P) decided to hold a voter education rally in the all Black fairgrounds, and have the then *hot attorney*, Floyd McKissick as the keynote speaker. Mr. McKissick succeeded James Farmer as president of the Congress of Racial Equality, and he lived in Durham, North Carolina at the time. To my shock and surprise, in the follow-up meeting at the Ambassador's Club, Howard Hunter went into a rage and said, "If McKissick came to Hertford County, he would turn all the white votes away from him because he had gone up and down Main Street in Ahoskie and the white folk said they would vote for him." We were shocked at his remarks because history indicated that the worst white man was preferred over the best Black man. Present at the meeting was H.D. Cooper, the principal of Ahoskie's Black high school, who was also a member of my church. He also stunned me by echoing Howard Hunter's words.

I heard that the N.A.A.C.P. and chair of PAC were at a stalemate with the sentiment of the meeting to cancel the rally and not let Floyd McKissick attend. I persuaded them to not let Mr. McKissick attend and the rally flopped. Even though the rally didn't materialize, Mr. Hunter was shocked to learn that the white vote he thought he'd receive never came. He lost as well as Reverend Hart, even though Hertford County was predominantly Black in its demographics..

The bright side was that even though Hunter did not win, he was next in line. He came in sixth out of a five member seat, and one of the Board members stepped aside because of sickness. This meant that Howard Hunter became the fifth member of the Board of Education, and that was gratifying to us all.

I should add that his wife and her side of the family were all members of my church. Reverend Hart, after a year, eventually became a member of the County Commissioners. They were among the first Blacks to serve in an elected office since Reconstruction, when the Ku Klux Klan ran all the Black voters off the polls.

Black Candidate for City Council

We then took note that all city councils that ran our cities were all white citizens. Therefore, we pushed ahead to run a Black candidate, Mr. Clarence Shaw Newsome, for City Council. He was a well-known school teacher and one of four outstanding sons of Mrs. Irene Yates who also was a school teacher and a very powerful woman of our church. Her oldest son Hawley Newsome was a veteran and school teacher; the third son Lewis Earl Newsome, ran his own mechanics shop and the youngest Carl Newsome, lived in Wilmington, North Carolina. Mrs. Yates came from one of the most outstanding families of that area, the Jenkins/Tyner family.

Well, needless to say, the City Fathers got another Black by the name of Buxton Harrell, to run as a way of guaranteeing the elections of their candidates. This way we could not *single vote*. I heard that Buxton was being considered by the white merchants to run, so I went to him and asked him personally whether he was thinking of running and if he would support Clarence Show's candidacy. He said, "No," he was not running and that he would support Clarence Shaw's candidacy. It was only when Buxton said he wasn't running that Clarence Shaw threw his hat into running for the Ahoskie City Council.

This was a conflicting situation for me as a pastor because both belonged to my church, and I was the pastor to both of them. Needless to say, both men lost the election. The following year, Roy Marsh, who was a well-known Black barber, ran for the Ahoskie City Council and won.

Grandfather of John L. Scott

Grandparents Coffers and Olivia Scott, Enfield, North Carolina

Rev. Scott's parents

Cousin who enrolled Scott into Bloomfield College

On the grounds of Bloomfield College and Seminary

Community residents bringing free food to Bertier County

Rev. Scott's first pastorate, New Ahoskie Baptist Church

Returning form Selma, Alabama, George Hall prepares to address
the freedom marchers at New Ahoskie Church

Wedding of Minnie and John, July 15, 1972

Sons, (l to r) Jerome, John, Jr , and James Augustus II

Dome of the Rock in Jerusalem

Herb Daughtry and Scott broadcasting from Riverside Church radio station

Breadbasket pushes fight against A&P (l to r: Amiri Baraka; Rev. Jesse
Jackson; Rev. Dr. W.A. Jones; Rev. John Scott, and Rev. C. E. Nesbitt)

Prayers on Courthouse Steps

Fighting to Better Economic Plight of Black People

Rally against A&P Supermarkets, New York City (l to r: Rev. Scott, executive secretary to Rev. Abernathy; Rev. Ralph Abernathy; James Brown, and Rev. Dr. W.A. Jones, Jr., president of Greater New York SCLC Operation Breadbasket)

Rev. Scott with Al Sharpton (c) and Percy Sutton (r)

Eightieth (80th) church anniversary speaker Dr. W. Franklin Richardson, pastor, Grace Baptist Church, Mt. Vernon, New York, and chair, National Action Network, with Scott

Rev. Scott with Representative Charles Rangel

Rev. Scott with Rev. Dr. Pastor Calvin Butts, Abyssinian Baptist Church, New York

Rev. Dr. W.J. Shaw, former president, National Baptist Convention

Second edition of *Feminist Theories and Feminist Psychotherapies: Origins, Themes, and Variations* (Harrington Park Press, 1997).

The Haworth Press, Inc., 10 Alice Street, Binghamton, NY 13904-1580.

Cover design by Marylouise E. Doyle.

Library of Congress Cataloging-in-Publication Data

Enns, Carolyn Zerbe.
    Feminist theories and feminist psychotherapies : origins, themes, and diversity / Carolyn Zerbe Enns—2nd ed.
        p. cm.
    Includes bibliographical references and index.
    ISBN 0-7890-1807-1 (case : alk. paper)—ISBN 0-7890-1808-X (soft : alk. paper)
    1. Feminist therapy. 2. Feminist theory. I. Title.
RC489.F45E56 2004
616.89'14'082—dc22

                                            2003022211

Feminist Theories and Feminist Psychotherapies
Origins, Themes, and Diversity
Second Edition

Carolyn Zerbe Enns, PhD

The Haworth Press®
New York • London • Oxford

Feminist Theories and Feminist Psychotherapies

Origins, Themes, and Diversity

Second Edition

More pre-publication
REVIEWS, COMMENTARIES, EVALUATIONS . . .

"**D**r. Enns has outdone herself in this second edition of her important book. It's not unusual today for students of feminist therapy practice to encounter the field without a clear understanding of the roots and heritage of feminist practice, which can lead to misperceptions and misapplications of feminist principles. Dr. Enns gives us an important, invaluable historical overview of feminist practice. Her book allows readers to see the organic processes by which feminist practice developed, and to appreciate the depth and complexity of what is meant by the term 'feminist.' The revision of this book to include sections on global and postmodern feminisms and their impact on feminist practice are particularly valuable to the seasoned reader. Enns' willingness to continue to challenge herself and her readers to expand their definitions of 'feminist' and 'feminist practice' is an important part of keeping the field alive, vital, and responsive to our roots as agents of social justice and social change."

Laura S. Brown, PhD, ABPP
Professor of Psychology,
Argosy University, Seattle

"***F***eminist Theories and Feminist Psychotherapies* is an insider's guide to thirty-five years of North American feminisms and feminist therapies. Dr. Enns' capacious, astute, and inspiring overview of feminist therapies takes us from the rambunctious, rebellious 1960s to the present. Her gracious eclecticism highlights continuities and connections among the diverse therapeutic practices inspired by North American feminism thought. Intended for feminist practitioners, the book steers clear of psychological jargon, high theory, and psychobabble. It invites feminist psychologists to ponder our theoretical, philosophical, and ethical commitments, as well as our practices. It deepens our appreciation of our history and awakens us to vibrant possibilities of a global feminism of the future.

If you enjoyed the first edition of *Feminist Theories and Feminist Psychotherapies,* you'll welcome this expanded and thoroughly updated version."

Jeanne Marecek, PhD
William Rand Kenan Professor,
Swarthmore College

The Haworth Press®
New York • London • Oxford

Rev. Scott with New York City Councilman Stanley Michels (l) and district
leader Alan Blumberg (r) of the West Side

Rev. Scott with Robert M. Morgenthau (l), Manhattan district attorney, and
Willie Dixon, director, Wilson Major Morris Community Center (r)

Rev. Scott with Dr. Keith A. Russell, director, Doctor of Ministry Program, New York Theological Seminary and proposer of this book project

Crozer/Barbour Reunion Dinner

Standing l to r: Rev Charles Booth, Rev Dr. Frank Tyson, Archie Leymore, Rev. Scott, Rev. Malachi Roundtree;

Sitting: Rev. Dr. Harold A. Carter, Sr., Rev Albert Prince Rowe, Rev Marvin McMickle (President, Colgate Crozer), Rev. Dr. J. Wendell Mapson, Jr., and Rev. Benjamin Whipper, Jr.

CHAPTER SEVEN

THE ANTI POVERTY PROGRAMS

First Protest Rally

During this time, following the Civil Rights Bill of 1964, Lyndon Johnson continued to carry out John F. Kennedy's dream of an anti-poverty program, which was controlled by the Hertford County Commissioners. The program was contrary to the anti-poverty guidelines that required that 51% of a board be 51% below the poverty line of $3,000. The County Commissioners called their group the Choanoke Area Development Association (CADA). It was comprised of four counties or resembled a geographical area larger than the state of Rhode Island

For some reason unknown to me, I was contacted by Sarah Yearbin and Jim McDonald from the "North Carolina Fund" in Durham, North Carolina. They questioned me about a possible rally at the National Armory in Woodland, North Carolina, and about how the anti-poverty program was handled by the commissioners.

We had several meetings at the First Baptist Church, in Rich Square pastored by the Reverend C. C. Lawrence. He became incensed that we were taking on the area rulers and forbade us to meet at his church any further because he said our job was "to work with white folk who knew best." The counties were all predominantly Black and this was part of the Black Belt of Eastern North Carolina made up of twenty-one counties out of one hundred counties that made up the counties of North Carolina.

The rally was eventually held outdoors in front of the National Armory in Woodland, North Carolina. I presided over the rally and Howard Fuller, who was a fiery orator, was the keynote speaker. Woodland was a small town of about only one hundred people. However, the rally drew over two thousand people. It was widely covered by the local newspapers. *The Hertford County Herald and The Virginia Pilot,* attacked his speech.

> Fuller's gestures in his speech when he threw up a white handkerchief as a symbol of what CADA brought to the area. However, the handkerchief symbolized nothing, other than to have hired only three staff people. There was a white director, Fred Cooper, the Black deputy, John Taylor and the Black secretary Betty Jean Boone of Murfreesboro, North Carolina. That's what the gesture entailed. When Howard Fuller threw a white handkerchief into the air, it conveyed the idea of a white "hoax", which represented a farce, with the intention of doing nothing educationally, politically, or economically for the four county areas. Choanke Area Development Association (CADA), had up until that time not met with any grassroots local people, in any of the four local communities throughout the four county areas.

No one knew how Fred Cooper and the staff were chosen by the commissioners although they were well known in their respective communities. Fred was an amiable and cordial individual who always appeared reasonable. They had not conducted any surveys of the needs of the area at all, and that is what caused such a dramatic outburst from Howard Fuller. The Hertford County Herald Newspaper was very critical and condemning in their coverage of the anti–poverty rally because it was like an "uprising" by the local people. But we were not discouraged nor dampened in our determination to make CADA responsive to the needs of the local communities.

Neither at that time, had the local "grassroots" leaders developed any overall organization in the four county areas. We were people from the local N.A.A.C.P Chapter and local community improvement groups, and that was the size of it. Some of us, if not most of us, had never met local leaders from outside our local counties or in our counties at large. This was a "eureka moment" that just lit up the minds of the concerned local Black citizens and a few pastors, who were mostly officers and leaders in our local churches.

In rural communities and small towns, the churches were from where the leadership came. Most of them were credible, responsible, outstanding people, or else, the newspapers would discredit our action, if it was led by people of suspicion.

With the encouragement and recommendation of Sargent Shriver we next met with George Esser who was a "bell ringer" for us. We previously worked with four North Carolina Federal Staff people. They were: Jim McDonald, Sarah Yearben, Howard Fuller and Willa Cofield. Willa Cofield, wife of Reid Johnson was from the outstanding Cofield Family of Enfield, North Carolina.

The Cofield Family was outstanding because they were highly respected Black leaders and business men in the Enfield and Weldon Communities. There were five brothers who were all successful and industrious. One was a well-known landlord in the Enfield Community, who was Willa Cofield's father; he not only sent his children through high school but onto college. His sons became some of the first college graduates of the area. The most noted one was Augustus (Gus) Cofield, the famous and well-loved Funeral Director of Enfield and Weldon. He had a Triple AAA Business rating and was an outstanding community leader. "Gus" Cofield worked with the local N.A.A.C.P. of Weldon, North Carolina in cooperation with a fearless Black lawyer, named Walker. Gus Cofield and Lawyer Walker decided to take the case of voter intimidation suppressing Black people in Halifax County, all the way to the Supreme Court, prior to the Selma to Montgomery "March over Voter Intimidation". They hatched a scheme to have Lawyer Walker go to Littleton, North Carolina and confiscate the voter regulations from the office of a third grade registrar and take them to Gus Cofield's office, and Lawyer Walker did. The police trailed him all the way to Weldon, and he was arrested and eventually took the case to the U.S. Supreme Court. It did not stop registrations and the "powers that be" from intimidating and denying Black folk from voting.

Gus Cofield also ran for the office of State Assemblyman in North Carolina Congress against the powerful Attorney Lunsford Crews, from

Roanoke Rapids, North Carolina. Gus didn't win although the Black population of Halifax County was about 60% Black. Many citizens were sharecroppers and tenant farmers and they were afraid to vote fearing economic and physical violence from white landowners. Once you were put off the land, no other white farmer would allow you to work for another farmer. Blacks were still in slavery; economically, educationally and politically. The only difference was that they were not owned legally. Educationally speaking, many weren't able to finish school. They were forced to stay home and work the land, as early as the third grade, but especially by the 8th or 9th grade. So the Cofields were symbols of "Black pride" and business success.

We were truly ecstatic! Rev. J. A. Felton became a local "think tank wonder" in our fifty-five member delegation. He had not been so seriously blended in the group before, but now he became a spokesperson for our loosely held fifty-five member delegation which included Alice Balance from Bertie County, several from Hertford and North Hampton Counties and Reverend Jeremiah Webb and Rev. I. A. Dunlap from Halifax County. We left it up to Felton to contact the North Carolina fund in Durham, North Carolina. He called and informed them of the day and time we were going, including the major networks of CBS and NBC as well.

Reverend Felton was an imaginative person, full of ideas and progressive ways of thinking. He contacted the television network in Durham, by telephone. I am sure, as well as the local *Hertford County Herald* Newspaper. He had no special contacts, so I presume, when he first called, he told whoever took the call that we were coming. We just took off on faith, and sailing in the wind, not wanting to waste a minute.

Meeting with Sargent Shriver

The Reverend J. A. Felton was a fearless school teacher and community activist.

He informed us that there was a schedule of hearings on rural poverty in America being held in Washington, D.C. chaired by Sargent Shriver. Everyone knew Sargent Shiver, the Facilitator. He was the brother-in-law of John. F. Kennedy. Fifty-five of us went to the hearing by automobile and took along a video showing the rural areas consisting of the poor housing and living conditions of the Choanoke area. Sargent Shriver was so impressed by our efforts that he applauded us for spearheading one of the best efforts of organizing the rural poor in America. Then he directed us to visit his good friend George Esser. Esser was the Director of the North Carolina Fund, which was founded by Governor Terry Sanford, who once ran for president of the United States.

Called Communists

Upon our arrival back to our several counties, the Hertford County Herald labeled us as "communists" and "Viet Cong Guerilla Fighters" against America in the war in Viet Nam. These were death threatening remarks. Nevertheless, the next week, without an appointment, we headed to Durham, North Carolina and the headquarters of the North Carolina Fund, for a meeting.

When we arrived back from the hearing on rural poverty in Washington, D.C., we were again shocked and frightened by the way the local newspaper, the Hertford County covered our presence at the hearing. The journalists continued to call us names like "Communists" and compared us to Viet Cong guerilla warriors, during the war in Viet Nam, South East Asia.

We were portrayed as unpatriotic when all we were doing was exposing the poverty in the rural areas, the economic plight of the people of the Choanoke Area and the need for better housing. We were frustrated by being attacked by the newspapers, and stereotyped as anarchists and trouble makers. In addition, we were disheartened and somewhat apprehensive about possible threats to our lives and possible bodily harm by the Ku Klux Klan and the violent element in the white community. Nevertheless, we marched full speed ahead. It was indeed remarkable and extraordinary how people from the four counties "jelled" into a mighty force and a marching army.

The Founding of People's Program on Poverty

We decided to have a sit-in at the North Carolina Fund in Durham, North Carolina. Shortly after we arrived, Director Nathan Garret came in and said, "We can't entertain you because your group doesn't have a name." So about thirty-five of us told him to leave the room and return in fifteen minutes, and we'd have an official name. As promised, we called him back and to his greatest surprise we presented him with the name "People's Program on Poverty" (P.P.O.P.). We also provided names of our various officers. The Reverend C. Melvin Cressy, President, the Reverend J. A. Felton, Director and myself as Chairman. We then set up the goals for each of the four counties which were: housing, voter education, social services and youth recreation.

They agreed to fund us to the tune of $165,000 for all the staff with the headquarters to be in Rich Square in the PA Bishop Building, Rich Square, North Carolina. The PA Bishop Building was the largest Black owned two-story building in Rich Square. It was once owned by a powerful local Black pastor, the Rev. P.A. Bishop. Although deceased, he made a lasting impact in the area and the General Baptist State Convention of North Carolina. While, these were some of the most creative moments, they were also very stressful because we were developing leadership in an area that never before formally established officials in the Black community. We were providing community and county leadership across the Counties that were never before displayed as a collective force for good. We were way ahead on the thinking of actions of the County Commissioners, the Boards of Education, City Managers, Mayors and white elected officials. There was *no* Black elected official in any of the twenty-one predominantly Black Counties. We were paving the way for community improvement and human betterment for all.

The Montgomery Movement

One Saturday morning, someone knocked on my door, and when I opened it, it was George Hall, Carlos Brown and Gus Chavis. Carlos and Gus said that they had persuaded George to join the Montgomery March after "Bloody Sunday," if I agreed to pay his way out of the N.A.A.C.P.

Funds. I was the president of the N.A.A.C.P. and the authorized person, who signed all the checks for any expenses. Naturally, I gladly agreed because after "Bloody Sunday" when the police on horseback trampled the marchers while praying on the Edmund Pettus Bridge (now the Hosea Williams Bridge), I knew that I was not going. To send George Hall was an answer to my prayers.

A good point of history to remember is that the Montgomery Movement consisted of three marches, all of which took place in March of 1965. The first on March 7th became famously known as "Bloody Sunday." This is when six hundred marchers were attacked by racist state and/or local police, dogs and water hoses. Dr. King didn't waste any time following this disaster and organized the second march on Tuesday March 9th. For this march, King appealed to the local citizens and Black clergy everywhere to come out. The television images of police brutality and cruelty comprising the events of "Bloody Sunday" were still fresh on the minds of T.V. viewers, so the turnout was tremendous. King scheduled the third march for March 21st. Thousands of sympathizers participated including Jews, Latinos, and Asians as well as known whites. National reporters covered the story and the event was the news item of the day.

We put in the local newspaper that George Hall, Sr. was going as a marcher from Hertford County to join in the march from Selma to Montgomery, Alabama. We knew for anyone watching that this was one of the bravest acts that a citizen could take by going to Selma because of the gravity of violence unleashed against "freedom fighters" in Selma, and other states in the South. People were beaten by white mobs with "Billy Clubs" and sticks. Reverend James Reed, a Unitarian minister from Boston, was beaten and stomped to death on the streets of Selma.

George was our fearless and brave representative. When George got back, he was greeted with an over flowing audience at the New Ahoskie Church, and gave one of the greatest speeches of his life. It was really a good speech. George by the way was a lifetime member of the Pleasant Plains Baptist Church of Winston, North Carolina located on the famed "Highway 13." (This was the highway where all the land for eleven miles from Ahoskie to Winston, was owned by Black Folk). He was also a trustee of his church and as a result of his great speech; he was chosen to follow my two years in office. He became the president of the

Hertford County N.A.A.C.P. which was the beachhead for social change in Hertford County.

Lawsuit against Local Hospital

Later that same year in 1965, George's sixteen year old son George, Jr., became ill and needed to be hospitalized at Roanoke Chowon Hospital in Ahoskie. The hospital was still segregated to our great surprise.

They placed George, Jr. in the hallway of the colored section because they said there were no more available rooms in the colored section. George contacted me and asked if I would file a federal suit against the hospital because it was receiving "Hill-Burton Federal Government Funds. I wanted to file a lawsuit because it was common knowledge that any facility receiving federal funds couldn't discriminate. I said that I would attempt to file a lawsuit and met with Reverend Felton from Greenville, North Carolina. He was the N.A.A.C.P.'s Legal Defense Fund Representative. I was mindful that Mr. Blanton, the hospital administrator was the cousin to the Reverend Dr. Sankey Blanton, President of Crozer Seminary, my alma mater, when I first went to him. I was consciously aware that to file a lawsuit against Dr. Blanton's cousin might incur Dr. Blanton's scorn because I didn't know where he stood on civil rights or on integration, for that matter. Neither Dr. Blanton, nor any of the faculty, ever spoke about the injustices and cruelties heaped on Black people. So I decided on being a little cautious in attempting to use "moral persuasion", which might succeed and maybe filing a suit against the hospital wouldn't be necessary.

When I spoke to Mr. Blanton., the hospital administrator, I told him that I didn't want to file the lawsuit, because by law the hospital couldn't deny *colored* patients access to rooms anywhere in the hospital. His face turned red as he said, "Preacher, if you think I'm going to endanger the health of white people by putting coloreds in their room, you got another thought coming." To this I replied: "You already have colored folk in rooms with white patients and they are whiter than you. I know because they are my church members." Nevertheless, we filed the suit and the following day, the headlines on the front page read, "Preacher Files Suit Against Hospital." On the opposite page was the heading, "The

Askew Family Donates $200,000 to Roanoke Chowan." This was an attempt to show me up as a destroyer of the hospital. This large donation was possible because the Askew Brothers of Harrelsville, North Carolina were wealthy landowners. They kept their money in the family by never marrying and lived with their sister who also never married.

In the meantime, Dr. Joe Dudley Weaver, a Black physician, heard about the lawsuit and approached Howard Hunter. He tracked me down with his walkie-talkie in order for me to meet with Mr. E. P. Brown, Chairman of the Hospital Board and the President of Georgia-Pacific Lumber Company Headquarters in Murfreesboro. Mr. Brown was a millionaire and perhaps the only millionaire in the entire county of Hertford, so it was important to meet with him.

Mr. E. P. Brown got Dr. Weaver to get us to agree to meet with him in the segregated restaurant, the Red Apple that was owned by E. P. Brown. The restaurant was closed when we met, so white folk could not see Black folk entering a segregated white restaurant. All four of us met with E. P. Brown. Carlos Brown, Gus Chavis, George Hall and the Reverend J. A. Felton. We presented our demands to fully desegregate the hospital and to publish the agreement in the local newspaper. We didn't imagine that they ever intended to implement the agreement. The hospital remained segregated and we filed the suit with the N.A.A.C.P. Legal Defense Fund. Within, a month they immediately desegregated. I regretted having to take such a drastic measure and I went back to check on Mr. Blanton to make sure he was all right. To my surprise, he greeted me with a smile and said, "Thanks preacher for making me do what was right. If I had done it on my own, they would have run me out of town." During this time, there was a move in the General Baptist State Convention (GMBC) led by the Reverend Dr. E. B. Turner, First Baptist Church of Lumberton to name me Director of Christian Education. This was the third highest position among Black Baptist Ministers in North Carolina. The organization was comprised of 1900 Black Baptist churches and 300,000 Black Baptist members.

I could only serve in the position for one year because it was too much to pastor and run all over the state at the same time. So I resigned as Director of Christian Education of the General Baptist State Convention of North Carolina (GMBC). My resignation was met with a cold response from the Reverend O. L. Sherrill, the Executive Secretary of GMBC, Reverend E. B. Turner of Lumberton, North Carolina and advocates. Turner wanted me to move up and eventually take over from the Reverend O. L. Sherrill, Executive Secretary. However, Sherrill never allowed me to get close to him as our Convention head and I didn't have the heart to take him on anyway. Therefore, I went back to my first love as Pastor of the New Ahoskie Baptist Church in Ahoskie, North Carolina.

At this time, in the spring of 1968, following my resignation, I received an invitation to become a "Ford Fellow" of the Urban Training Center for Social Change in Chicago. The program was headed by the Reverend James Morton, who in 1970 became the Dean of the Cathedral of St. John the Divine Episcopal in New York City.

Becoming a "Ford Fellow" to study at the nationally renowned Urban Training Center for Social Change, was quite an honor for a small town preacher coming from a town of about 7,000 people. But I must say that in Ahoskie we had a cadre of people committed to social change not only in Ahoskie, but also in Hertford County and the entire Choanoke area.

The P.P.O.P Movement captured the complete attention of the entire state of North Carolina. We set up branch offices in each of the four counties with Reverend Jeremiah Webb, Reed Johnson and Wilma Johnson from Halifax County. Using my own money along with Gus and Eleanor Davis and Dimples Newsome, I set up our own office on Maple Street, just one block from Main Street in Ahoskie. Then Reed Johnson proceeded to try to stimulate recreational activities for the region. Rev. J.A. Felton worked on housing and eventually built C-2211-D3 low incoming housing in Ahoskie. This was surprisingly supported by the Ahoskie City Council and all of our activities were built around the local churches in the area including voter education.

Also at that time, Governor Wallace was a candidate for president of the United States of America. We served notice on the city and county fathers that Wallace would never carry our country. We were successful in his defeat.

I volunteered my time for all the activities, but the following year, the Voter Education Project of Atlanta, headed by Vernon Jordan, paid 15 cents a mile for the voter education drive in Hertford County.

I remember at this same time that the Rev. S. P. Petteway of Lewiston, North Carolina in Bertie County and the Rev. F. L. Lagarde of

Edenton led a march from Edenton, North Carolina to Windsor, North Carolina. They were accompanied by a throng of five hundred marchers, dramatizing the need to bring free food to Bertie County. Bertie County was the poorest county in North Carolina and the 33rd poorest in the nation. When Rev, Petteway, the marchers and I arrived in the Town Square of Windsor the County Commissioner heard of the march and attempted to break it up. The state troopers charged into the marchers as we were crossing the Chowan River Bridge. However, we had everyone kneel down on the bridge in a peaceful and submissive way, so that the marchers would not be incited to leap over the rail and into the river. When the troopers saw that the marchers didn't budge, for no apparent reason, they walked over to a teenager in the group and jerked him up in a forceful manner.

When the trooper jerked the sixteen year old young man to his feet, we yelled to everyone: "Stay down, don't move." They intended to start a stampede, but we remained still as the troopers placed the young man in a car and drove him away alone by himself

We were afraid for him and feared for his life, because we remembered how the police and local people of Mississippi killed fifteen year old Emmit Till. The footnote is that the trooper who went ahead of us released the young man in the town of Windsor where we were headed.

The march from Chowan County to Windsor was eight miles away. When we arrived in Windsor, it was noon on Saturday. We went in and met with the County Commissioners and they agreed to take "free food" to the county. When Rev. Petteway addressed the crowd in the Town Square from the second floor balcony of the Municipal Building, he was supposed to inform the crowd of the decision that was reached. Instead, he pulled a trick and introduced Mr. Bazemore, the chairman. As Rev. Pettaway introduced him he said, "Mr. Bazemore will tell you of their decision." Whereupon, the stoic Commissioner cursed and said, "Damn that Petteway!" Then he proceeded in informing the marchers that they would be filing for "free food" to arrive in Bertie County, and it would be available by the next month.

By this time Mr. Golden Frinks was the field secretary for S.C.L.C. Mr. Golden Frinks of North Carolina came to me and said that he had a proposal for the training of farm workers who had been displaced and that he wanted us (P.P.O.P. members) to sponsor the proposal through the anti-poverty program. He knew that the commissioners would not touch it if they knew that the proposal came from him. Frinks was like a lightening rod for a change. He got the officers of P.P.O.P.—Rev. J.A. Felton, George Hall, Gus Chavis, Dimples Newsome and Rev. C.M. Creecy to meet with Mr. Melvin Johnson in his home. Johnson who was initially from Winston, North Carolina worked with the Office of Economic Opportunity. He said that he liked the idea for the displaced farm workers and he thought he could get it funded for the displaced farm workers in Eastern, North Carolina. Johnson said that he would meet with us again upon his return from Washington, D.C. We were inspired and encouraged that hopefully he would do something for the displaced farm workers.

When Melvin Johnson met with us the second time, he said that he had to bring C.A.D.A. in on the implementation. C.A.D.A. was our adversary and the arm of the big land owners. Yet, we agreed that we could jointly work together, only to later discover that Johnson had betrayed our trust and had given our proposal over to C.A.D.A. The organization still had done nothing for the area and only had the same three staff people. We were furious and wanted to go to Washington to block the whole idea. However, after some analysis we determined that we were only trying to help the Choanoke area—that the most important thing was not whether we were given credit, but whether or not the people would be helped. The proposal was funded for thirty counties of eastern North Carolina and Rev. J.A. Felton eventually became its first director. The program became the Rural Cooperative Association (R.C.A.) located in Rich Square, North Carolina.

Rev. C. A. Hart asked me, "Why don't we go to the Commissioner to bring in 'free food' for Hertford County." We went to the Hertford County Commissioners and made our appeal, and without a hitch they agreed. To this Rev. Hard replied, "Thank you for what we are about to receive."

Black Woman Beaten by Police

In the course of events, on our way to the North Carolina Fund in Durham, North Carolina we heard that a Black woman was beaten unmercifully by the police in Murfreesboro, North Carolina. We had to do something about it. I told the people to meet us at City Hall that same night when we arrived from Durham, North Carolina. When we arrived at the meeting room of the Murfreesboro City Council, the room was full and Rev. Felton was in the midst of describing what happened. No action was taken by the officials of the town. Therefore, I sought help from J. Levonne Chambers of the N.A.A.C.P.'s Legal Defense Fund, which was located in North Carolina, (Chambers later became the National Director of the N.A.A.C.P. Defense Fund in New York and eventually the Chancellor of North Carolina Central University in Durham, North Carolina).

Mr. Chambers sent an attorney by the name of Ferguson (who later became a Federal Judge) to represent our petition against the Police Department. We found out in the process that the police took the woman to Dr. Joe Dudley a Black doctor, in Ahoskie for treatment. The outcome of the visit wasn't learned, because the doctor never said a word to anyone!

On the other hand, we heard that the woman's wounds healed, and she went on her way in a humble and meek manner. The events of that incident were a common occurrence in rural and small towns. The police roughed up local Black citizens and threatened them, whether or not they appeared resistant to their abuse.

Mt. Nebo Church is burned

In 1967, during the time of the series of burnings, one of the most outstanding Black churches was burned to the ground. It was Mt. Nebo Baptist Church on Highway 158 located on the outskirts of Murfreesboro, North Carolina. Reverend C. Melvin Creecy was the pastor and he was a very controversial pastor in the county at that time.

Reverend Roland Pruitt, the then pastor of the First Baptist Church in Murfreesboro, called and asked me why we didn't lead a drive to help re-build Mt. Nebo Church. We held a county wide fund raising rally and donated the money to the church's pastor. He suffered personal attacks for his civic action, and the superintendent of the Mt. Nebo Baptist Church Sunday School called me crying and said, "That was why their church got burned down, because McCreecy was messing with them white folk when he was told to leave them alone." Of course the police officer who investigated the fires determined that there was no racist motive to setting the fires. Instead, it was the determination that the person who set the fires was a pyromaniac and mentally unbalanced.

Anyway, when we met Attorney Ferguson with the City Attorney, Mr. Jones the policeman was indicted. Before the officer was sentenced, someone in town began setting fires all over town. We never dreamed that it would be the same police officer! He was detected because he left town after the fires and traveled toward the Chowan Beach area. Another officer on duty stopped him and asked him to open his truck. There he found the evidence—cans of kerosene and rags used to set the fires. The sad part of the story is that when the convicted officer was jailed, he committed suicide.

In 1967, I was invited to attend the Urban Training Center for Social Change in Chicago. To undertake this, I first drove two hours from Ahoskie to the Raleigh/Durham Airport. Then I flew to Chicago each Monday and flew back every Friday evening to attend to my pastoral duties at the New Ahoskie Baptist Church in Ahoskie, North Carolina. I met fellow activists from the nation and studied with a Reverend Luckie. I also met with a Reverend Carol Felton who was initially from Elizabeth City, North Carolina and formerly headed the Voter Education Project for the Black Belt—the 21 counties of Eastern, North Carolina. At that time the Voter Education Project consisted of twenty-one predominantly Black counties in North Carolina.

In our first week in Chicago, it was required that we take *the plunge* as it was called. This required living on the streets of Chicago as a "homeless" person with only $5.00 for three days and nights. I had on overalls, a baggy cotton shirt, a beat up jacket, brogan shoes and a beat up hat to stand against the cold on the streets. I was attempting to appear "homeless" on the streets, trying to make it the best way I could.

The first night we got put out of the 5 and 10 cent store when we tried to get the clerk to look at us seriously and see that we were not "bums." She refused; instead she felt that we were hustlers from the streets trying to beat her out of her candy.

For supper, I ate a hot dog and drank a glass of milk. For a place to spend the night, we got put out of the bus station and decided to go to the twenty-five cent movie theatre and sleep on the cushioned seats. However, we were thrown out of the movie theatre and were again on the streets. Finally, we heard that Reverend Clarence Williams from Brooklyn, New York had a room in the Sheraton Hotel. It's beyond me as to how we were able to get inside without being detected. However, about twenty of us crammed into this one room for the night. The next and final night, I convinced the clerk at the Y.M.C.A. to let me spend the night there.

While I was in Chicago, I came across a well spoken "homeless" person. After I gave him a quarter, I learned that he was once a Seventh Day Adventist preacher. I asked him, "How did he end up on the street as a beggar?" He replied, "I just can't seem to get over the hump."

Rev. Martin Luther King is assassinated

Dr. Martin Luther King was assassinated on April 4, 1968 in Memphis, Tennessee. When I returned to Chicago that following Monday, many of the streets were smoldering from burned out buildings. Daley was the Mayor of Chicago and he gave orders to *shoot to kill all arsonists* and *maim and cripple* all looters. His words stayed with me.

That Monday night the word got out that Stokely Carmichael was speaking at a huge theatre. I attended along with two white Catholic priests. Jesse Jackson also spoke but when the President of the Black National Rifle Association spoke, he led the 3,000 strong in a chant, "Kill, Kill, Kill." The white priests thought they should have left. I said, "Never in your life, we'll get stomped to death! If anyone says anything to us, tell them you are Black, and that the white man raped your mother!" Hell, the place was fever pitched and it was surprising that a riot didn't break out that night.

Garment Workers

During the summer of 1969 the International Garment Workers Union (I.G.W.U), attempted to organize the largest factory in Ahoskie. The union sought my help in trying to break the stronghold the company had on the workers for fear of losing their jobs. I helped out by letting them meet in the Fellowship Hall of New Ahoskie Church. Certainly I agreed, in order that the workers would receive "just wages," overtime and double time, as well as health insurance and decent healthy working conditions. The meeting was made up of 99% whites and a few coloreds, along with the union organizers. At the close of each meeting we would join hands and sing the union song, "Solidarity, Solidarity, the Union Makes Us Strong." I knew that I had Ku, Klux, Klan members in the meeting. But it didn't matter to me because they were all working for the same cause—just wages, health insurance and decent working conditions. The effort to organize failed.

At the same time I was told that the largest lumber mill in the area was not paying minimum wage, overtime or double time. So I invited the Director of the Labor Department of North Carolina to Ahoskie and sued the plant. I only said, "Don't forget to give something to New Ahoskie Church because without the church, I wouldn't be pastoring." This was my condition on the workers receiving back pay. When they got their back money, which was in the thousands, they did like the nine lepers and failed to return and even say, "thank you."

Elected Co-Pastor in Chicago

I can't forget that while I was in Chicago, I met the Pastor Reverend Bob O'Dean of the Garfield Park Baptist. He said that his congregation demanded to have a Black assistant on board, and would I consider taking the position? Well, Chicago was fascinating and so I met with the search committee and then returned to Ahoskie. I was eventually called to co-pastor and was offered all of the benefits that were afforded an American Baptist minister. I met with my board of deacons of Ahoskie, who asked me not to leave. They said that I had more work to do. After further prayer, I was led not to accept the call to Chicago, and stayed on at New Ahoskie Baptist.

CHAPTER EIGHT

JERUSALEM

Visit to the Holy Land

In 1971, when Rev. Jones decided to take his congregation of Bethany Church on a six-day Holy Land Tour, I was invited to go along. I didn't have the money, but he made it possible with the complimentary tickets he received from friends.

There were forty of us, including Rev. Leroy Jefferson, a Union Theological Seminary student who was his assistant at the time; and his oldest children: Billy, 20 and Beth 9. Their travel along with Rev. Jefferson (Jeff) was also paid for with complimentary tickets.

We lodged in the King David Hotel in Jerusalem and shortly after our arrival where we were met by Abed, our Arab Christian tour guide. He was the most resourceful, informed individual who assisted us in getting the most mileage out of our six day visit.

We toured Old Jerusalem, the Valley of Gethsemane and the Church of the Holy Sepulcher, on the site where Jesus rose from the dead. This site is known as Gordon's Tomb, where there is a crack in the rock, from an earthquake that occurred in the First Century. We walked the "Way of the Cross," the Via, Dia-la-Rosa where Jesus bore his cross and a Black man Simon of Cyrene helped him carry it. Each day in 1971, the Israeli Army marched through the streets in Old Jerusalem, which was

98% Arab and shouted, "Ho, Ho, Moshe Dyan!" Dyan was the military General who defeated the Arab nations in the 1968 war.

We traveled down from Jerusalem in Jericho (17 miles), as soldiers stood on the hillside with weapons drawn. Hostilities were still simmering between the Arab Nations over the *occupied territory*. We also waded in the Jordan River and visited the Ancient City of Jericho where I believe, John the Baptist preached in the wilderness. We viewed the archeological site of the city of Jericho where the people are dark and olive in complexion. I was surprised to see brown and dark skinned people when pictures of the Holy Land only shows Caucasian like features. We also visited the Kum Rum Caves, where the *Dead Sea Scrolls* were found.

I knelt at the shrine where Jesus was born in the basement of the Church of the Nativity, and managed to get a picture of this scene. We prayed at the "Wailing Wall," the grounds underneath, are the remains of King Solomon's Temple. Above the grounds we visited the "Dome of the Rock," initially known as Mount Mariah, where Abraham, was to sacrifice his son, but an angel spared Isaac's life.

We toured the grounds of the McCabean Revolt where the Jews revolted against Roman rule and where all the Zealots were killed. We sailed across the Sea of Galilee and embarked on the grounds where Jesus gave the *Sermon on the Mount*. I could write volumes on this visit, but space does not permit it. I will only conclude by saying that it was a spiritually unforgettable, memorable experience for which I will be eternally grateful to Rev. Jones.

CHAPTER NINE

THE BREADBASKET YEARS

Hired to Head Breadbasket Operation

Following this trip, I was extremely flattered, when my dear friend Dr. Jones, asked me to come to New York City to head the S.C.L.C. Breadbasket Office of Greater New York. He was the Chair and the Reverend Herb Daughtry was the Vice Chair. I held out for a month, but in September of 1969, I tendered my resignation to the congregation and joined Jones (as I called him) to work for the economic empowerment of Black people. It was the fourth phase of Dr. King's movement and the slogan was, "Your minister fights for jobs and rights."

Dr. Harold A. Carter, buddy of Dr. Jones, preached my final revival. The following week I packed up my gear and in a U-Haul van hitched to my Buick Electra, I headed north.

Ahoskie: My First Love

As I reached the top of the Delaware Memorial Bridge, I never dreamed that parting from my beloved Ahoskie could be so traumatic. There was no going back; I was only going forward into the world of New York that I never knew, like Abraham of old, and by faith I had to believe I could make it.

Before I left Ahoskie, I paid all of my bills. To my surprise some of the residents in the white community who had never encouraged me said, "Preacher whether you know it or not, you've done this community a lot of good." Mr. Early, the postmaster of Ahoskie even made the same comment.

New York: Operation Breadbasket

When I arrived in New York, Bill Jones had already established the S.C.L.C. Bread Chapter in Greater New York. The year was 1968 and there were some nineteen major chapters established nationally. Dr. King was the recipient of a grant from the Ford Foundation used to call activist pastors nationwide to Miami, Florida. Dr. Harold A. Carter (the licentiate when Dr. King pastored at Dexter Avenue Baptist Church in Montgomery), and Bill Jones were present along with other ministers who were: Reverend Wyatt T. Walker, Reverend Abernathy, Reverend Joe Lowry, Rev. E.K. Steele, Reverend Fred Shuttlesworth and Reverend Harold Carter and other clergy and leaders in the Civil Rights Movement.

My salary was paid by the S.C.L.C. Foundation, which was headed by Attorney Chauncey Eskridge, who was also Muhammad Ali's lawyer. Jones had already met with some activist pastors who were mostly from Bedford Stuyvesant in Brooklyn. He had also dealt with some of the companies in the Bread Industry such as: Tastee Bread and Wonder Bread. Their method was to establish covenants of equity in certain categories establishing a "Covenant Agreement" such as:

1. Have a certain percentage of Blacks on the Board equal to our patronage;
2. Have them put a certain percentage of their deposits in Black and minority banks;
3. Have a certain percentage in top management;
4. Have a certain percentage of service advertising with Black and minority advertisers;
5. Have a certain percentage of philanthropic support for "Black worthy" cases and put ads in Black and minority newspapers.

Jones and his team were in the process of dealing with the "Bottle Industry" when I arrived. Key members on the team were: the Reverend Clarence Williams, Reverend C. E. Nesbit, Reverend L.P. Taylor, Reverend Ed. Wharton, Reverend George Murray, Reverend Roland Nyman, Reverend Clifford Johnson and others. Jones met each Saturday with the ministers at 9:00 A.M. for breakfast at his church Bethany Baptist Church in Brooklyn, New York. There they would strategize, layout and finalize their plan for action. Their plan was as follows:

- First, inform them by getting the E.E.O.C. report on a company as to their make up of Black workers, from top to bottom.
- Second, meet with the president of the company regarding our findings and make demands, with an agreed upon period of compliance.
- Third, demonstrate against a company by pulling a boycott if they did not meet with our demands, including leaflets, picketing and boycotting in order to bring them to the negotiating table.
- Fourth, a Covenant of Agreement between the company and Breadbasket would sign in mutual agreement that the companies would improve their employment of fairness. Usually the process would take about three months; sometimes it would take longer if a company stalemated.

The preachers met only with presidents who were the persons of power. We did not meet with their subordinates, only with the president.

Pepsi Cola & Coca Cola Bottling Company

Reverend Jones and the team negotiated with Pepsi Cola Bottling Company which had their headquarters in New York, to meet with A. Kendal, president of Pepsi. He was the former Chairman of the Election Committee for President Richard M. Nixon. Pepsi Cola was the only Fortune 500 Company that had a Black Vice President. His name was Fitzhugh and he was a former professor of economics at Howard University. Needless to say, the negotiating went along smoothly and an eventual contract was signed with Pepsi Cola.

Breadbasket Office

Jones secured the second floor, rear of the Carver Bank at 1271 Fulton Street in Bed Stuyvesant, Brooklyn for the headquarters' office. And on October, 1969, we celebrated with the ribbon cutting ceremony with Reverend Jesse Jackson, National Director of S.C.L.C. in attendance. Reverend Gardner C. Taylor gave the prayer and together Reverend Jones and I, held the scissors and simultaneously cut the ribbon, ceremoniously opening the first official S.C.L.C. Breadbasket Chapter office in New York. The nationwide Board members at the time were; Reverend Wyatt Tee Walker and Reverend George Lawrence, of Antioch Baptist Church in Brooklyn.

A service of celebration was held one block away from the new offices at Friendship Baptist Church, 12 Herkimer Street, where Reverend Uriah B. Whitfield was the pastor. The Reverend Jesse Jackson was the keynote speaker and Mahalia Jackson was the soloist. I must say that it was an impressive night.

Following Pepsi Co., we began negotiating with the Coca Cola Co., on 34th Street on the East Side Highway. A Mr. Millard was the president at the time. He was a very cordial person with whom to negotiate. We signed a covenant and, decided after three months to do a review.

Negotiating Strategy

When in a negotiating session, if we ran into a conflict or an impasse, or if there were differences within the team, we never disagreed with one another openly during the negotiations. We called for a break and caucused until we came to agreement privately.

If pressure needed to be applied, Reverend Jones had Reverend Edward Wharton to be the "hatchet man", predicting the worse kind of response on our part. This meant picketing and boycotting, which was geared to offset a company's margin of profit, which most could not afford to lose.

Canada Dry

After signing a covenant with Coca Cola, we moved on to Canada Dry located at 100 Park Avenue in New York. Our negotiations seemed to go smoothly but we unexpectedly ran into a snag.

The Equal Employment Opportunity Commission (E.E.O.C.)

The snag was the percentage of Blacks compared to whites. Historically, the percentage of Black employment centered on "Black males." When we went to Canada Dry for the first time, the E.E.O.C. report included females, Asians and others. We were astounded because the report gave an 18% minority employment rate, but upon inspection, Black males were scarce at best. We felt duped by the government because the struggle had historically obtained jobs for men. We knew that we were going up against a stone wall. Therefore, since our patronage was 20%, we demanded 30% in our negotiations. The company agreed to our demands across the board without a hitch, after we enlightened them that there were several slices of the economic pie.

Breadbasket Chicago

One of the first things I did when I was hired as Executive Director, of S.C.L.C. Operation Breadbasket was to visit the Breadbasket's headquarters in Chicago.

The Reverend Jesse Jackson was the National Director, Reverend Calvin Morris was the assistant, and the Reverend Willie Barrow was the Secretary.

It was exciting getting acquainted. I also met with the late Attorney Chauncey Eskridge, who was the Chair of S.C.L.C.'s National Foundation. Cirillo McSweeney was the Treasurer.

Chicago's Breadbasket Rally

Jesse's Saturday morning Breadbasket rally was activism at its best. Ben Branch, a saxophonist, led the Breadbasket Choir and the now famous musician Quincy Jones was the choir Director.

Usually there was an hour for rally time, which led up to Rev. Jackson addressing the rally. The rally was made up of community organizers, officers of the community, civic, social, political and fraternal organizations, a cross section of workers and leaders in the Chicago area. By the way, it was Ben Branch to whom Dr. King made his last request to play "Precious Lord." And this was the night of the rally in Memphis—the night before he was shot and killed.

When I went to Chicago straight from North Carolina, I went dressed in the typical style of a preacher: white shirt, Black suit and tie, whereupon Chauncey Eskridge looked me up and down and said, "When you get back to New York, get you some "Bell Bottoms." I laughed, because I obviously wasn't dressed in the style of that time.

While in Chicago, Reverend George Murray, traveled with me to Chicago, and accompanied me to entertainment night of Black EXPO. The famous African singer Odessa was the premier soloist of the evening. Also on the program were the Jackson Five and Redd Fox. He was the comedian who almost put me in the hospital with a joke he told about a Black Baptist deacon who prayed for Governor Wallace.

He started out with, "O, Lord, bless Governor Wallace. Let him come down with an unbearable stomach ache; bless Governor Wallace! And Lord, when the ambulance comes, let them fall down carrying Governor Wallace to the hospital! O Lord, bless Governor Wallace! And on the way to the hospital, let the ambulance have two flat tires, bless Governor Wallace! When they operate, let them operate with two *rusty* knives, bless Governor Wallace. And Lord, when they bury him, let him be buried in the deep end of the cemetery, where all that muddy water can run into his grave, bless Governor Wallace." He spoke in the prayer medium of the old Black deacon, and it was hilarious.

Coming back to New York I saw the need to broaden our coalition from the few preachers around breakfast, to incorporating other community, religious and civic organizations.

"The Welfare Rights" groups from Brooklyn became a part of our coalition because, if we ever boycotted, we needed *troops* and they were the largest activist groups in Brooklyn and Manhattan. As a matter of fact, there were over 17 Welfare Rights Organizations headed by a popular social worker who organized welfare chapters. He later suffered an early and untimely death. I also accompanied busloads of Welfare Rights Groups to Albany when Nelson Rockefeller was the Governor, and I spoke at the Albany Mall along with other speakers. This was at the time when the legislation for better welfare benefits was passed.

Breadbasket Rally-Brooklyn, New York

With the rapid increase in members, it was no longer practical to limit Saturday morning just to a breakfast. The gathering now rose from about seven preachers meeting to about 70 to 80 people easily. Reverend Jones was somewhat resistant to the enlargement from the first preachers to a large coalition because he feared our efforts would be diluted and side tracked. I was able to show him a great teaching moment for the attendees, which he was capable and able to comprehend. He consented and the "Breakfast" became a "Breakfast Rally" instead of "Breadbasket Breakfast". Then we tried building a Breadbasket Choir with the singer Eddie Kendrix, and another musician by the name of Professor Herman Stevens. He was one of the musicians who played at the funeral of James Cleveland. The choir never quite got off the ground.

The Reverend Al Sharpton

Around 1970 when Reverend Sharpton was a teenager in high school, his mother asked Reverend Jones to take him under his wing in order to mentor him as a father figure and give his life more exposure. Reverend Jones immediately appointed Reverend Sharpton to head the Breadbasket Youth Division. This was an unusual move on her part, because Sharpton came out of the Washington Temple Church of God in Christ, under the charismatic leadership of a very popular broadcast preacher, the Late Bishop F. D. Washington. His mother saw that

Sharpton would get greater exposure and be guided by the most activist preachers in New York, if not in the entire nation. Sharpton fell right in and was able to accomplish many things.

Sealtest Ice Cream

My job as Executive Secretary was to call the president of a company that we decided to target and to request a meeting concerning their "fair employment" practices in the Black community. The front office would often try to give us the *runaround* but our policy was that the preacher would only meet with the president. We eventually agreed upon a meeting in the Board Room of the company with their president and his team.

Many times before we met, they'd want to know who the ministers were or who made up our community of ministers. We'd give them only the names of Reverend Jones the Chair and Reverend Herbert Doughtery, Vice Chair. My job was to be up at 5:00 A.M. and begin reminding the negotiating team of our meeting with the company. This was usually in the early morning hours, no later than 10:30 A.M. Most pastors were free during the morning hours, because most pastoral duties were the heaviest in the afternoon and evening hours.

Our first meeting was in the Board Room of their office building. Our second meeting was at Bethany Baptist Church. This church was a huge gothic structure where the company could feel the weight of the Black community as it was conveyed through the presence of the Black preacher. By the way, it became normal usage to call us "Black" now, since the Rock and Roll singer, James Brown, made it popular in his song, "Say it Loud, I'm Black and I'm proud."

Race Terms

Most of us grew up being called "Colored", or the more formal term "Negro." *Black* was the term that was usually used as a negative, but with James Brown's song, "Say it Loud, I'm Black and I'm Proud," blackness took on a rich cultural and racial meaning probably for the first time in recent history. Black was no longer a negative but a term of pride. It was during this time that the "Afro Hair Style" also became nationally popular, along with the pearl handle "Afro Comb." Men stopped processing their hair, which was the process that gave them that slick look.

Malcolm X

Malcolm X had a tremendous impact on overcoming the meaning of "blackness."

Afro features became emphasized and dashikis were popularly worn by many of the Civil Rights Leaders, especially the Black Panther Party and S.N.C.C.

Once in my sophomore year, someone invited me to a Malcolm X meeting in Newark. I was always curious to hear outstanding speakers of the time, as I was an inquisitive eighteen young man. When I heard Malcolm X speak, I was enraged by the truths that he told. I knew that if I went to hear him again, I would end up hating white people, although I was taught by my mother not to hate them as they hated us. According to her, two wrongs didn't make a right. So I decided never to go listen to him again. It was not what he taught, but about what he said, and the way he said it, calling white men the *devil*. If I continued attending his lectures, I would have undoubtedly quit college. There was no way to separate his words and my exposure to the white faculty and students I dealt with on a daily basis. Knowing that I was the only Black student on campus, there was no way I would be able to continue my education with Malcolm's words etched in my memory. I was determined to not let anything get in the way of my college education, so I never attended another lecture. The Malcolm X depicted in the movie by Spike Lee is a fictional character. He was not a mild man.

After a month of negotiations, we eventually signed a covenant agreement with the Sealtest Company. The components of the covenant agreement outlined the following:

1. Discussing our findings with the company
2. Presenting our demands for greater fairness; and finally

3. Setting a three month time for compliance. Usually a company was not in full compliance after three months but, if they showed progress in increasing the percentage of fairness across the board, Breadbasket would eventually let them have only a year to be in full compliance.

Martin's Department Store

In the fall of 1970, it came to our attention that Martin's Department Store in Brooklyn had a disproportionate Black employment rate based on our patronage, so we planned to pay them a visit.

In our first meeting we met with Wilbur Levine, President and the Vice President of the department store. They became very incensed over being accused of "sins" against the Black Community because of unfair employment practices. They had no Blacks on their Board of Directors in addition to the following"

- No money in Black banks;
- No advertisement in Black newspapers;
- Only a few Black service contracts; and
- They only gave meager gifts to Black causes in comparison to what they and all other companies did in the white community.

In the initial meeting they refused to negotiate in good faith; therefore, we announced from our pulpits to start an economic withdrawal from Martin's Department Store.

We developed a fact sheet and distributed it to all who came to shop at Martin's. Reverend Timothy Mitchell, the Pastor of Ebenezer Baptist Church in Queens, was quite demonstrative and vocal in our picket line in front of Martin's downtown in Brooklyn. After a week of daily picketing, Martin's President said he was willing to sit down and negotiate with us around our differences. Mr. Levine was quite a negotiator and after several sessions a covenant between Breadbasket of Greater New York, was finally signed in a mutually agreed session. It was a cold day in the month of September, but under the leadership of Dr. Jones we shook hands as we parted and promised to review their progress in three months.

At the end of the three month period, they made one Black person a department manager and improved in other areas. Things were developing so fast that we didn't have time to even go back. We just hoped that after a company president made an agreement the same would happen with other companies we were dealing with due to the threat to keep them moving towards equal employment practices.

A & P Supermarkets

The A & P Supermarket Chain became our next target. In 1971, A & P was a 5.7 billion dollar corporation, headquartered at 460 Lexington Avenue in New York, around the corner from Grand Central Station. We received information from a reporter at Life magazine that A & P had over 500 stores throughout the metropolitan area and had only two minority managers working for them. One was Black and the other was Hispanic. In addition:

- They had a 75 member Board of Directors, with no Blacks;
- No advertising in the Black media;
- No deposits in Black or minority banks;
- No philanthropy to Black colleges and universities;
- Only a few service contracts with Black entrepreneurs.

We attempted to meet with Mr. William Kane, the President who refused and instead sent a Mr. Tom Nonaan, Director of Public Relations to meet with us. Of course, this was unacceptable, because we only met with the President (and his Board Members, if needed), the person with the power to make decisions on behalf of the company.

It was clear that we had run up against a "brick wall" so to speak. We decided to have a press conference at the Overseas Press Club at 40 West 40 Street, and announced an all-out nationwide boycott through the Associated Press, CBS and NBC. A & P's margin of profit was less than ½ of a penny profit. The Black community's margin of patronage was at least 30% of their sales. So we met in Dr. Jones' study until 1:00 A.M.

strategizing, planning and conferencing about the press conference; because we planned to march from the press conference to the Graybar Building and have a sit-in until the President met with us.

Our strategizing team members were: Rev. John Henemier of St. John Lutheran Church; Father Thomas Keane,, of St. Peter's Claver Roman Catholic Church and other clergy including the Reverend Herbert Doughtery, the then Reverend C. E. Nesbit, of Bethesda Baptist Church in Bushwick, Brooklyn, Reverend George Murry, Pastor of Mt. Pisgah Baptist Church, the then Reverend Roland Hyman, Bethelite Baptist Church, and the then Reverend L. P. Taylor, Pastor of Glover Memorial Baptist Church.

Prior to the A & P Boycott, we built up our support organizations to over seventy which included the Catholic Archdiocese of Brooklyn and Long Island, the Roman Catholic Archdiocese of Manhattan, the Episcopal Diocese of New York, the Vulcan's Society (the Black Police Benevolent League), the Welfare Rights Organization of Brooklyn, Manhattan, the Bronx and the Union of Reformed Rabbis in the U.S.A.

Also joining us in the build up of our action against A & P was the heir Huntington Hartford. He also owned Paradise Island in Nassau, Bahamas. He was most supportive and felt that A & P had become too monolithic and not contemporary enough, particularly when A & P had the opportunity to own the Xerox Corporation but opted out of the negotiation.

Prior to our takeover of A & P Headquarters, we held a major rally in Bethany Church. All of the major networks were present. *The Brooklyn New Yorker* and *The Amsterdam News* faithfully covered all of our efforts. The major newspapers like *The New York Times, The Daily News and The New York Post* did not; although *The Daily News* was the only major newspaper to cover our first Black Business and Professional EXPO and the action against A & P.

As a result of the Reverend Jesse Jackson being the Keynote Speaker for the rally, the house was jammed with supporters. Jesse infuriated Operation Breadbasket's local attorney Clayton Jones with his statement, "I will not leave New York until I have met with Williams Kane, the president of A & P." Yet after the first day of the sit-in at the A & P, Jesse left and returned to Chicago. In fairness to him, at that same time Jesse was embroiled in a controversy with Mayor Richard R. Daley, so Jesse had to first take care of his home front so as to keep the peace.

The Press Conference

On the following day, we announced our nationwide boycott against A & P at the Overseas Press Club, located at 40 West 50th Street and Fifth Avenue. We the ministers of S.C.L.C. Operation Breadbasket of Greater New York gave our "Fact Sheet" to the press and stated our case. Reverends Jackson, Abernathy, President of S.C.L.C and Jones led the procession from the 40 West 40th Street location, then down 42nd Street past the Grand Central Terminal Complex. We were followed by the press, Bill Murray as well as Gil Noble, the dean of Black journalism. It was a cold windy day with snow flurries in the air. Nevertheless, we bundled up and braved the weather.

When we entered into the lobby and went directly to the 9th floor of the A & P building, the security guards were paralyzed when they saw the clergy, ministers, priests and rabbis arrive. They looked like the prison guards when Jesus rose from the grave. Reverend Freddie Brunswick held the door open with one hand and preached from the Bible with the other hand. We proceeded to the office of William Kane and took it over. There we sang, prayed, preached and rallied to the glory of God. Reverend L. P. Taylor preached, "I saw the dead, great and small, standing in the judgment to be tried." It was an *epiphany* as well as a Theophanous moment. In my estimation, nobody but God could have gathered us into the Graybar Building and the president's office of the A & P but God, without a hitch or incident.

The Arrests

We occupied the office for three days, whereupon wave after wave of picketers and protesters were arrested and hauled off to jail. Reverend Abernathy was in the first wave of arrests. He was the most disrespected by the ABC News pressmen. When a cameraman almost hit him in the face, Abernathy asked: "If I were Martin Luther King would you badger me like this?" The rudeness and disrespect continued even though our protest was nonviolent and peaceful.

Later on Reverend Dr. Harold Carter, of Shiloh Baptist Church in Baltimore joined us in the sit-in. We were hauled off to jail and placed in isolation. As we slept on hard board benches, lights were kept on all night. Reverend C. E. Nesbit, Pastor of Bethesda Baptist Church in Brooklyn, preached on "Daniel in the Lion's Den." The next morning we were given sweet tea and a dry cheese sandwich. That was it. One of the Catholic priests became ill to his stomach and Reverend Dougherty laid hands of deliverance on the brother and his stomach was cleared. The Lord set free the evil spirit that tried to inhabit his stomach.

Upon our release, we were led up to Criminal Court on Lafayette Street in Manhattan and awaited trial. There were about 200 of us ministers, priests and rabbis. Mrs. Jones mother of Reverend Jones, Jr., came from Kentucky and joined us in the courtroom, and began to hum the old Negro spiritual, "O, Lord, Have mercy." God did have mercy on us through our attorney, Clayton Jones, and Judge William Thompson, who got Mayor John Lindsay to commute our sentence. We walked out of court free and thankful to God for our temporary victory in that we did not have any penalties hanging over our heads.

We never met with William Kane, the president of A & P, but the store immediately implemented changes in their practices. For example the changes were:

- Attorney Hobart Taylor, the legal counsel to President Lyndon Johnson, became the first Black to serve on A & P Board of 75;
- Monies were placed in Freedom and Carver Banks;
- Black advertisers received ads for their papers;
- More Black and Hispanic managers were hired;
- Philanthropy was given to Black colleges and causes;
- Service contracts were granted to Black contractors.

Overall it sent a message to all the major Fortune 500 companies that they were accountable for fair economic and employment practices in our communities, based on the patronage from our communities.

Breadbasket had developed several divisions since its inception in 1968:

- The Youth Division, headed by Rev. Al Sharpton;
- The Businessmen's Division, headed by Ben Wright, Vice President of Minority Markets at Clairol Corporation located on Park Avenue in New York;
- The Legal Arm Division headed by attorney Clayton Jones, brother of Rev. William Jones;
- The political civic committee headed by Percy Sutton;

The other side of dealing with our rightful share from major corporations was the development of Black businesses.

One of the most prominent emerging Black media outlets was the magazine *Black Enterprise*, founded by Earl Graves. We all admired Earl Graves because he once worked in the Justice Department under the late U.S. Attorney General Robert Kennedy.

Robert Kennedy

Robert Kennedy was instrumental in developing the "Model Block" Housing Program in Bedford Stuyvesant, Brooklyn along with Urban Formation and Earl Graves was involved in both. As I reflect, it was Robert Kennedy who was elected from Bed Stuyvesant as a U.S. Senator, and ran as the presidential candidate in this position. Other members of the Businessmen's Division were:

- Howard Dabney, Manager, Carver Bank, in Brooklyn;
- Leon Wright, President of the Brooklyn Jaycees;
- Dameon Kinnebrew, owner of cleaning firm;
- Von Blaine, food company president;
- Percy Sutton, Head, Political Action Division;
- Ophelia Devore, Founder President, the Grace Del Marco Agency,;
- Earl Lewis, Founder, *Essence* Magazine;

- Among others, most notable was Ben Wright, twin brother to Episcopal President of Fr. Nathan Wright, of Newark, New Jersey;
- Media Consultant from *Time* Magazine.

We decided to have a "Black EXPO" of business and professional organizations. It began on Thursday, November 4 through Saturday November 6, 1970. The location was the Statler Hilton Hotel on 33rd Street and Seventh Avenue, across the street from the famed Madison Square Garden

Black EXPO

The Ribbon Cutting ceremony was held in the lobby of the Statler Hilton Hotel.

In attendance were Percy Sutton, Borough President; Kenyatta of the Mau Mau's and former bodyguard to Malcolm X; Reverend Jesse Jackson, Reverend Jones, Reverend Herbert Doughtery, Reverend Al Sharpton, Bishop F. D. Washington and I.

Reverend Washington prayed the opening prayer, and what a prayer! Reverends Jones, Jackson and I cut the ribbon. It was a classic event with over 200 major corporations displaying their products along with Black entrepreneurs and other entertainment celebrities.

The EXPO opened each day at 10:00 A.M. and closed at 10:00 P.M. Over 200,000 attended and on Saturday November 6th the last day, participants stood four deep and a block long trying to get into the exposition. However, Dr. Abernathy was able to get in with his press secretary.

James Brown

James Brown was the featured entertainer for the evening, along with other entertainers. They all performed without charging a fee, as long as Breadbasket covered their expenses.

Clayton Jones booked all the entertainers and handled their expenses.

Initially I was signing checks for Black EXPO but there were so many to sign that I could not keep up with them, so I told Reverend Jones that I could not sign any more checks, particularly since Ben Wright needed someone available immediately when he required checks signed. So Reverend Jones asked his brother Clayton to work with Ben Wright in handling all future expenses. We needed to expand the workload as I was already dealing with the corporations which were stressful enough. Anyway, we closed Breadbasket "Black EXPO on a high note. It was the first major Black business and professional exposition held in New York.

The Awards Luncheon

The Breadbasket Awards Dinner later followed at the Commodore Hotel which was located above Grand Central Station in Manhattan, on 42nd Street between Madison and Vanderbilt Avenues. The Hyatt Regency Hotel has since replaced the Commodore Hotel.

Clayton Jones chaired the awards luncheon with the help of Betty Brooks, former secretary to Harry Belafonte. There were twenty five outstanding Black Achievers selected from around the world. Among them were, Julius Nyiere, President of Tanzania, Percy Juleon, noted scientist; actor Ryan O'Neal and others. The Reverend Dr. Eugene Callender, President of the Urban Coalition chaired the event. Callender was the former host of the telecast *Positively Black.*

The dinner was to begin at 8:00 P.M. with hors d'oeuvres served between 7:00 P.M. and 8:00 P.M. However, to our shock, Betty Brooks, who was our secretary, had the programs and couldn't be found or contacted. We waited until 8:30 P.M. and decided that the luncheon would proceed without a printed program. I don't recall if the programs ever appeared. All I remember is that it was said that Betty Brooks choked under the magnitude of the Awards Luncheon as the event became too overwhelming. Nevertheless, it was a grand evening. We hoped that out of the "Black EXPO" and the Awards Dinner, we would reap enough profits to hire an additional secretary and be able to purchase a station wagon in order to carry all the ministers as we traveled from place to place. To our utmost surprise, we ended up financially in the hole, because too many tickets were given to outstanding celebrities and personalities, and instead of a profit, we faced a deficit. Nevertheless, it was an historic occasion. And the Daily News gave Breadbasket a two-page centerfold covering the event.

In the midst of all these frantic activities, Reverend Jones still maintained our regular Saturday morning Breadbasket rally where reports, complaints and observations were shared. The highlight was an economic, philosophical and Biblical speech by the Reverend Jones. Furthermore, we always closed the morning with the famous Jesse Jackson chant, "I am somebody. I may be poor, but I am somebody. I may be unemployed, but I am somebody. I am Black, and I am somebody."

We didn't like the "Black" part at the time because it appeared to be apologizing for our " ness." However, it usually was the closing chant, and we broke up and went our several ways. Ministers went to prepare for "Sunday Morning" and to put their finishing touches on their sermons. I usually went home to my apartment, where I lived on Lenox Road, in Flatbush, Brooklyn. Once there I made contacts and also prepared to be the guest preacher for the Sunday morning service in some church.

Dick Cavett

The famous saxophonist Roland Kirk came to one of our Saturday morning meetings and stated that there were only a few "token" Blacks working in the entertainment and T.V. networks.

We decided to invade the stage of one of Dick Cavett's shows in order to bring to bear our Breadbasket protest. At that time the only visible Black entertainers were: Pearl Bailey, Lena Horne, Eartha Kitt, Harry Belafonte, Sidney Poitier and the Breadbasket protesters. We all wanted Black representation on all networks, not on just a token few. So, one evening, about five of us rushed onto the stage of the Dick Cavett Show. We were surprised that Mr. Cavett did not jump up and leave the stage. Instead, he gracefully received us. He said that he understood our protest and he would use all of his influence to further open the doors for Black entertainers. A follow-up meeting was setup, but because of conflicting schedules, the follow-up meeting never took place, but at least our "message" was heard.

Gil Noble

As a result of our takeover of the Dick Cavett Show, Gil Noble invited Reverend Jones and I to discuss the plight and fight of ministers and entertainers to appear on all the networks and once and for all end the appearance of "all white" telecasts, when in 1971 Blacks and Hispanics made up over 30% of the city's population. The telecast, "Like It Is" regrettably appeared at noon on Sunday morning when the majority of Black folk were in church. Jones and I attempted to get the program scheduled for a later time like 2:00 P.M. at a time when most Black church goers would be home. Noble dealt with current issues of the day, many of which were edited out of his telecast for fear of offending white audiences. Eventually the program settled in at 1:00 P.M. on Sundays and has been a permanent program on the NBC Network for over forty years.

Loews Incorporated

Following our holding the Awards Luncheon, Loews Incorporated became our next concern. We were concerned about their fair economic and employment practices in their theaters and hotels, both in New York, and London, England. We met with the President R. Preston Tisch who was a very sociable person. At the meeting was his personnel manager, Cliff Benfield, the former president of Central Broadcasting Station (CBS).

They were very open and promised to honestly look at their E.E.O.C. reports and all Lowes' practices regarding the patronage of their company by the Black and Hispanic community. They were totally cooperative in every way possible to see that justice and equity were done in their company. Later on, we learned that they also owned the Lorillard Tobacco Company. Overall it was a smooth and cooperative negotiating experience that we had with Loews.

Robert Hall

We then turned our attention to the garment industry. We met with the President of Robert Hall and his Board of Directors. Their speech in the boardroom was "harsh and rough" when they talked about their competitors. It was the first time we observed a demeanor like this.

Our negotiations broke down with Robert Hall, and we came to the decision that the only way to make them come back to the negotiating table was to boycott the company. Boycott was always the "Secret Weapon" that was always in the background when dealing with a company that wouldn't negotiate in good faith. We regarded it as a SIN against our community to allow any company knowingly to exploit the consumer market of our people and never get our rightful share.

We always negotiated from the percentage of patronage from the Black community. If all our patronage was 15% of a company's business, we would demand that percentage across the board for our community, which had been discriminated against for decades. We were not trying to receive compensation for sins in the past but to transform the practices of a company in order that they would deal "justly" with our rightful share of each slice of the economic pie.

The Economic Pie

The common idea was that we wanted our rightful share of the economic pie but this was inequitable, when there are "several slices" of the economic pie and we demanded our "rightful share" of "each slice" of the pie.

Broadly speaking, the slices of the pie included:

- ✓ Our presence on Boards of Directors where policy was set:
- ✓ Our rightful percentage of vice presidents and department heads (usually Black people were at the bottom of the economic pyramid where the money was low and meager;
- ✓ Our rightful share of deposits in Black banks;
- ✓ Our rightful share of the advertising dollars;
- ✓ Our rightful share of philanthropy in the non-profit foundations;
- ✓ Our rightful share of service contracts (these are the major portions that make up the economic pie, that gives "longer life" to the dollar in our communities, that make a community healthy and strong, instead of anemic and frail).

Boycott Robert Hall

At the time we began the boycott against Robert Hall, Reverend Jones along with other clergy across the country were selected as "King Fellows." Becoming a fellow allowed them to pursue their D.Min., Degree by studying at Colgate Rochester Divinity School, in Rochester, New York and at the University of Lagos in Lagos, Nigeria. This left me "alone" to carry on the fight against Robert Hall.

The King Fellows

Under the professorship of Reverend Henry Mitchell of Colgate Rochester Divinity School in Rochester the King Fellows were:

- The Rev. W. A. Jones, Jr., Pastor, Bethany Baptist Church, Brooklyn
- The Rt. Rev. Canon Frederick Boyd Williams, Rector, Chapel of the Intercession Episcopal Church, New York
- The Rt. Rev. Wyatt Tee Walker, Pastor, Canaan Baptist Church, New York
- The Rev. Harold A. Carter, Pastor, New Shiloh Baptist Church, Baltimore, Maryland;
- The Rev. Floyd Massey, Pastor, St. Paul, Minnesota;
- The Rev. H. Beecher Hicks, Pastor, Metropolitan Baptist Church, Washington, D. C;
- The Rev. Samuel McKinney, Pastor, Seattle, Washington;
- The Rev. James Forbes, professor, Union Theological Seminary, New York.

It was in the heat of the summer, and I was joined by Reverend David Licerish, Assistant Pastor of Abyssinian Baptist Church in New York. Robert Hall eventually cooperated and we settled up with our grievances and the company.

Jesse Jackson

In the summer of 1972, hostilities rose against Jesse that carried over from the A& P sit-in. We met in our Black EXPO office in Manhattan to discuss what disciplinary action should be taken against him, because Jesse had incorporated the Chicago EXPO without the approval of the S.C.L.C. Board.

Clayton Jones was Jesse's nemesis. So in the meeting they decided to pressure Reverend Abernathy, the President to suspend Jesse as the National Director and not let Chauncey Eskridge be S.C.L.C.'s attorney, but instead use Clayton Jones as S.C.L.C.'s attorney in dealing with Jesse. Under pressure, Reverend Jones went around the room questioning us as to how others felt about the proposed action to be taken against Jesse. When it came to me, I said, "The day you remove Jesse Jackson as Director is the day you remove the head from the body, and the body can't live without the head."

Attorney Clayton became extremely angry with me, and asked that I be dismissed, whereupon I said, "Before I sell my soul for a mess of partridge, God will grow grass on Fifth Avenue before he will let me starve." Reverend Jones noticed how I felt, and asked if I felt that way would I remain silent. I said, "Yes."

The next week, they met in Chicago and Jesse was suspended. This was one of the darkest days in the life of Black America, because we had no one at the head with the vision, tenacity and time to carry on the fight like Jesse. Then as I prophesied Breadbasket which Reverend Wyatt Tee Walker named, became history. When I saw that, I knew it was time for my departure and to return back to the pastorate. I was already considering a new pastorate for over a year, and nothing had come through.

One day when Reverend Jones and I met, along with others, in front of the Time Life Building, we met an officer of St. John Baptist Church in Harlem. Reverend Jones had heard about the church and so he asked Dave Billings to get me a preaching engagement, and he did.

CHAPTER TEN

International Travel

Africa

In 1988, Reverend Carl Flemister, Executive Minister of American Baptist Churches, sponsored a trip to Africa which my wife and I were fortunate to be sent on by the church. We went from West Africa to Central Africa and ended the journey in Kenya in East Africa.

We left from Kennedy International on an Air France 747 flight with the needed immunizations. Our first stop was in Abidjan, Ivory Coast where we spent a day in the airport which was a shocking experience. The airport afforded none of the familiar restaurants or comfortable seating facilities we were accustomed to in the United States. This made for a very uncomfortable lay over.

The next stop was the day and night we spent in Dakar, Senegal where we stayed at the Novotel Hotel. In Dakar, we had a tour guide who took us through the streets in the midst of a lot of hustle and bustle. We saw a lot of over-crowded buses and local people striving to make it in the work-a-day world. While we walked, we were surrounded by beggars and peddlers peddling their wares and swarming around us like pigeons descending onto a morsel of bread.

We were bombarded by the peddlers until I said to the tour guide that I was returning to the hotel. The next thing I knew he had paid off the ringleader to back away from us and to no longer hamper our street travel. On the way to a local restaurant, we passed through a street that was inhabited mostly by lepers; and I never witnessed anything like that before. I saw people with their eyes almost eaten out by disease, and parts of arms and legs eaten away. It was a tragic sight. I thought that leprosy was done away with back in Biblical times.

Anyway, when we arrived at the restaurant, I noticed that a most expensive watch that was a gift was missing from my arm. It was a gift from the Pastor's Aid Ministry of St. John's so I immediately started to frantically look for it; but to no avail. Even though I retraced my steps, I never found my beautiful and expensive watch. It took me a long time to recover from such a treasured loss.

Then I understood why we were so surrounded by the peddlers. They probably only served as a shield for the "pick pockets" while they performed their trade.

The following day, we visited Goree Island, which was the last stop on the slave trade route, where there were holding pens, before being shipped off to South America, the islands in the Caribbean and eventually America across the Atlantic. This was called "The Trans-Atlantic Slave Trade."

The most humiliating experience for the "captives" was the underground "cellars" which were about two feet high, where the most difficult resistant slaves were kept, with the hope of breaking their spirit. Our tour guide said that he always wept when he took a group to Goree Island because the suffering of humans was unbearable. The most impressive site was the stately white wooden building of the church, where each person was baptized before crossing the Atlantic Ocean, This was done so that if anyone lost their life, their soul wouldn't be lost. What a mockery of "so called religion." That scene haunts me to this day, because I know that if I had been a captive I would have been housed in one of those cramped dungeons. The reason I know this is that every muscle and fiber of my being would have been in rebellion seeing my mother, father, sister and brother ripped from their home land and the villages from which they came.

We then took an Ethiopian Airlines flight to Abidjan, Ivory Coast where the restaurant manager in the airport convinced me to sponsor him to America, so that he could continue his education. I sent him the necessary papers but I never heard from him at all. I guess the mail was confiscated because the army guarded the mail at the airport to keep local people from taking it—especially correspondence from America.

We flew from there to Kinshasa, Zaire while Mobuto the Dictator was in power, and just killed several citizens who were mostly students found on his grounds. They were on his property to try to run him out of office.

After our arrival, we stayed at the Missionary Compound where the missionaries had their headquarters and then we left to go to the local villages. Since we were forty in total, we were divided into five groups. I chose to go out into the back country to see how the local people lived in their little villages. My group flew to Vanga by a local plane serviced by Christian Missionary Swedish pilots. We stayed at the home of a Medical Missionary from Illinois. They were very hospitable, and took us out to the local hospital, which was the only one for a hundred miles or more. The building didn't look like a hospital. It looked like military barracks in a war torn zone and was serviced by the Christian Organization of German Doctors. The building consisted of cement floors, cinder block walls and housed the barest equipment. There were people camped out on the grounds waiting for two to three days before they could be seen. There were children with yellow jaundice and bulging bellies due to hunger and malnutrition. I wanted to take pictures to take back to the congregation, but I wasn't permitted to do so. If I knew this was forbidden, I would have secretly carried a flash camera, to photograph and show the dire misery in which so many people lived. This way the church's missionary society could have sent monthly support. We tried to initially, but it was eventually overridden by needy situations at home and in support of our mission work back through the LOTT Carey Foreign Mission's work in the island, Guyana and also Liberia, West Africa.

We saw some of the work being done by Habitat for Humanity, which was President Jimmy Carter's work. We were guests of the Missionary Organization name ZEBCO (Zarian Evangelical Baptist Christian Organization) that was headed by a Ph.D. student at Union Seminary in New York.

We worshipped on Sunday with the local people. It reminded me somewhat of growing up as a boy with the "Brush Harbors," where we country folk fed our local guests after church when the service was over.

The church my group attended didn't have an offering table but a stand on which they placed their money and a handmade wooden pulpit. The group didn't have chairs, only blocks of wood on which they sat, but what a service! What singing and what a spirit of worship!

The largest church we visited was in Kikwit in the Bandando Province near Eboli where Pastor Muyamina was the pastor. The church was in a more standard building and it owned an electric generator and housed a large women's knitting society. The thing that shocked me most was a picture of a "white" Jesus hanging on the wall behind the pastor's desk. I asked Pastor Muyamina, was he aware that Jesus was a North African of possible brown complexion conducive to the people of that geographical area. He said, "Yes." I then asked him, how did he justify that white Jesus in the midst of 100 percent Black congregation members? He said, the Southern Baptists gave them the missionary money and asked him to put the picture on the wall. Well, I guess some people without a deep sense of integrity will stop at almost anythingin order to promote their cause. That was a teaching moment for him, and who knows, they may have agreed with him.

We were guests in the home of Vangu Lusaquano's executive secretary. We ate by daylight, and it was an adventure because there was noelectricity nor modern plumbing in the houses in Kinshasa. Water was obtained at the end of the street by filling up buckets. I admired Lusaquano because Rev. Calvin Butts of Abyssinian Baptist Church thought enough of him to sponsor him.

Eventually the entire group returned to the compound and the home of ZEBCO.

Rev. Flemister noticed that a lot of the compound supplies were from South Africa where Nelson Mandela was still in prison at the time on Robin Island. It was Mayor Dinkins, the Mayor of New York then who had all investments in South Africa reinvested elsewhere.

In a calm and diplomatic way, Reverend Flemister let the directors know how offensive that was to us as Africans and Latino Americans and they pledged moving forward, to boycott the supplies from South Africa.

After five days, we flew to Nairobi, Kenya where we stayed in one of the local hotels. We took a trip out to Senengetti, among the Masai, where they were mostly herdsmen, like shepherds guarding their castle.

We toured the Wildlife Reserve where we saw lions, elephants, wild beasts and other animals. Minnie and I stayed in the Ambaselli Lodge near Mt. Kilamanjaro which is the tallest mountain in Africa. Snow covers the very top even in the summer. We slept in a bed that was draped by a nylon curtain, which surrounded us from overhead and flowed down to the floor completely covering us as we slept. This way if a lizard or small insect fell towards the bed, it wouldn't fall on us.

We also toured the Harambi Museum which shows the original human species, the Neanderthal, Cro-Magnon man and the Java man who are supposed to be the species form which the human race originated from thousands of years ago.

We thought of going over to the Hilton Hotel which had the nicest display of fruit that your eyes could see and desire. We were warned many times not to eat anything that was washed in the local water and not boiled. Well, we were sure that we were safe. We were at the Hilton and like in the scene from Adam and Eve, we ate of the forbidden fruit.

I can't emphasize more on the marathon race we all indulged in going back and forth to the restroom the following day as we flew out of Kenya. That trip from Kenya, back to Abidjan en route to America, was a flight of a lifetime.

On returning to the States, I invited Lusaquano to sponsor a missionary workshop at the church. Our paths never crossed after that. I hope he is fulfilling his dream of helping his people in Zaire.

France

Every Sunday morning in Harlem, Black churches are flooded with tourists from around the world mostly from European countries and Australia. Of all the countries that visit St. John's on Sunday, 40 to 50 tourists are from France. Among the French was the Jean Pierre Houdin Family who stayed for the entire service. After service, they would stay, mingle and fellowship with the congregation. They were especially close to Deacon Thomas Canada and Mrs. Canada and their daughter Theresa who spoke fluent French. In January 1996, the Houdins very generously gave the Canada Family and Minnie and me a nine-day trip to France and an invitation to stay in their home.

The Houdins lived in the city of Bluoi, off the Bluoi River known as the Parish of the Castles. They lived in a three story mansion and gave us our own quarters in which to live. Jean Pierre was a wealthy trader in household supplies as large as Montgomery Ward. We toured his plant and all the workers seemed like one great big family. Jean had two drivers who drove us around throughout the day in his Mercedes Station wagon and took us wherever we wanted to go. We ate breakfast in their home each morning served by their Brazilian maid. Mrs. Houdin grew up with her family in the Ivory Coast where her parents were Medical Missionaries. She was a plain and simple person who shunned extravagance and purchased her clothes from "Goodwill Stores." She was a Buddhist.

We visited the castles during the day; the most notable was the Chambourg, built by Leonardo DaVinci, as the King's Hunting Castle for his guests and had 365 fire places. Although the draperies on the wall were over a hundred years old, they still looked freshly made. When Victor Hugo visited the Chambourg, he is noted for asking: "What madness envisioned such luxury and opulence?" We also visited the castle built by the King for his Mistress Madam Pompadour. This was a white stone marble castle that glistened in the sun, and was about 500 feet long and three stories high. Most of the castles we visited were still abandoned since the French Revolution in 1789. The most impressive Cathedral was the Cathedral built to honor King Louis XIV, featuring all the main points of his life from birth to military conquest engraved on the huge stained glass windows.

On our last day, we visited the massive Cathedral of Notre Dame, built in the 10th Century A.D. Photography doesn't give the structure credit or convey the awesomeness of the columns and structure. You just have to be there. As part of our final day, we dined at the oldest restaurant in Paris, established in 1789 where the French plotted to overthrow the King and execute Queen Marie Antoinette by guillotine. The French "Bill of Rights" written on the walls was still visible.

Our last event took place back in the City of Bluoi, where we feasted like a king and his court. On the menu were five servings of wine (I didn't drink any because I didn't travel that far to get drunk). An opera singer was flown in from Paris and a fabulous evening of entertainment ensued. Minnie's oldest brother Boogie, who was stationed with the U.S. government, flew in to spend the evening with us.

We departed the following day on a French 747 Airliner for a six hour flight back to New York. The trip still remains one of the most enjoyable ones of my lifetime. Thanks to the Houdins who still visit and worship with us on an annual basis.

CHAPTER ELEVEN

CALL TO IMMANUEL BAPTIST CHURCH

First Sermon

At the same time, a layman by the name of Herb Miller, on staff at the City Council of Churches, introduced me to the previously all white Immanuel Baptist Church, on Lafayette and St. James Place. The Reverend Dowdy was the Senior Pastor. The church was 99 percent Black and demanded a Black presence in the pulpit. I was called to Co-pastor with an office and all benefits. The salary was $10,000 annually, with M & M Insurance including disability, death benefit, travel and library expenses. Rev. Dowdy was charitable and kind, and welcomed me as the co-pastor.

I accepted the call to become Co-pastor and submitted my resignation in writing to Reverend Jones, with deep appreciation and respect for the opportunity of having served as Executive Secretary of Operation Breadbasket. Reverend Jones graciously accepted my humble resignation and wished me well. At the same time, I became engaged to Miss Minnie Watts, of Portsmouth, Virginia. Two years earlier, I felt it was time to marry, settle down and live a married family life. I don't know how Reverend Jones and all the other ministers pastored their churches and fought almost daily for the welfare and well-being of our community. However, I was about to learn.

The fist sermon I preached at Immanuel was entitled, "In Quest of the Highest." At the conclusion of the sermon, standing at the door with Reverend Dowdy was Persis Judd, wife of Federal Judge Orin C. Judd (the first person to rule against the Viet Nam War). She asked Reverend Dowdy what was wrong with the P.A. System. She said she couldn't hear me because I was too loud.

Well, that was a serious blow to my spirit. Thinking to myself I said," I had long since left the seminary where I was *acting white;* I had come through the Civil Rights fight where I had to be my *natural self,* with strong emotions and feelings." The whole worship experience of the "Black" was alien to Immanuel at that time. The hymns were dull and dry (dead) and I felt that the Holy Spirit was frozen in that church. Also, in the Fellowship Hall following worship, Dr. Judd eased beside me and asked, "Do you think there's enough room for you and Reverend Dowdy together." Well, I was intimidated because I am sure he wanted to hold onto the three or four whites left in the church. All around the church was the largest community of Co-Op buildings next to Starret City in Coney Island, where there was a sea of Black folk. I couldn't see myself staying to keep a church integrated when my concerns were to be Christ-centered and liberation-minded.

At the same time, I planned my wedding for July 15, 1972 and Immanuel was planning for my wedding reception at Pratt Institute. Charles Pratt, for whom the school was named, was a famous deacon in the early days of Immanuel Baptist Church and a contemporary of John D. Rockefeller in industry.

After much prayer and fasting, I met with the then Chairman of the Deacon Board and told him how I felt, that my mission was over. It was only three weeks later, and I knew that I didn't fit.

CHAPTER TWELVE

ST. JOHN'S BAPTIST CHURCH

Marriage

I received a call from St. John's Baptist Church in Harlem, in June of 1972. Shortly after this call, the Chair of the Deacon Board of Emmanuel Baptist Church called a meeting for me to share my decision to resign from the position of co-pastor at Emmanuel Baptist and go to St. John's Baptist Church in Harlem. It was a shock to them, and Deacon Fitz Henley said, "He'd never have respect for a minister again for having done what I did." I knew that I had made the right decision. As a matter of fact, when they called after I left, I recommended who they should approach as a Black Co-Pastor.

I understand that the Reverend H. Edward Whitaker helped them in the transition from being a traditional white church, to being a Black church in the community surrounded by a sea of "blackness". He was more on the meditational, teacher style. I was more of an evangelical and liberated person.

I was still living on Lenox Road in Brooklyn and moved to a larger apartment that was more suitable for my new marriage. In the meantime, The Chair of St. John's Trustee Board, suggested that my wife and I go to the parsonage after our marriage to get ready for our new arrival.

Minnie came from one of the most successful Black families in Portsmouth. She is the oldest girl of seven siblings—three girls and four boys, and a graduate of Norfolk State University and Lehman College.

Her father set a fine example for his children, as he was an independent business man who owned and operated the largest Black owned taxi company, which consisted of seventeen cabs. In addition, he was a noted bondsman. Minnie's mother was a homemaker who raised all her children, guiding them in the direction of a college education. Minnie and two of her younger sisters have a Master's Degree in Education.

Minnie's oldest brother Bruce is familiarly called "Boogie." His Master's Degree in Business Administration is from Hampton University. He also completed work on his Ph.D., and is a member of Phi Beta Kappa. He is a former employee of the Government's Purchasing Department. He is retired and lives in Florida. Her second oldest brother Ashley, is a graduate of Virginia University in Richmond. He served in the Navy and is retired from Allstate as a Claims Adjuster. He is married to Janice who is an E.K.G. Specialist and they live in Portsmouth, Virginia. Minnie's third brother Keith Oswald has a Master's Degree from Hampton University, and formerly taught in the Department of Business Administration at Virginia University. He is married to Marian who is also a teacher. They live in Richmond and are the proud parents of Keith, Jr. Her youngest brother Lemuel has a Master's Degree from Norfolk State University similarly to his older siblings Faye and Olga. He is a public school teacher in the Portsmouth School System and is married with one son. His name is Brandon.

Minnie's sister, Iris Faye Green has a Master's Degree and is married to Keith Green. Keith has a Master's Degree in Engineering and works for Newport News Shipbuilding and Dry Dock Company in Newport News, Virginia. They are the proud parents of one daughter, Lauren, who is a graduate of Hampton University School of Journalism. She followed in her father's footsteps and works in the public relations department of the Newport News Shipbuilding and Dry Dock Company. She is presently not married. Minnie's youngest sister Olga has a Master's Degree from Norfolk State and teaches mentally challenged students in the Portsmouth School System. She is also unmarried.

The Watts Family is known as one of the pioneering and successful families in the Tidewater area: one uncle was an attorney, another a dentist, an aunt was a florist and a great aunt was a nurse in the early 1900s. They are all remarkable blessings as they all worked hard and always had their own.

Our Wedding

I married Minnie Louise Watts on July 15, 1972 at the Historic Ebenezer Baptist Church in Portsmouth, Virginia. The Reverend Harvey Johnson, Pastor and the Reverend C. W. Cuffee, Minnie's pastor, officiated at our wedding. It was a glorious day! The reception was held in the spacious lawn of Minnie's home and was catered by a renowned catering company. Members of St. John's as well as my mother came from North Carolina. My brother Winston was the best man, and my youngest brother Lynn, was one of the five ushers. My sister-in-law, Atherene (Winston's wife) was also the Maid-of-Honor.

The Reception

The late Deacon Bembry, Chairman of the Deacon Board, and Philmore Williams prepared a big reception for us in the lower auditorium of the church. It was a warm and friendly reception where we met all the heads of the various ministries (which were then called clubs). I was amazed that city people could be just as warm as country people. It was a good feeling to be called back into the pastorate, because there was something about pastoring that truly touched the depths of my being.

As Minnie and I left the reception for the airport, Minnie's mother broke down crying, "Oh my daughter," and my mother followed crying, "Oh my son." We left for the airport in the brand new two-toned dark and light green Chevy Caprice that I recently purchased. We spent the night at the Norfolk Municipal Airport Hotel, and the next day we flew to the Bahamas. In the Bahamas, we stayed at the Paradise Island Hotel and Resort Center with the compliments of R. Preston Tisch, the owner of the hotel and the New York Giants.

Paradise Island was sensational with all of its amenities and was located on the ocean front. I thought my wife could swim since she was from Tidewater—the largest Bay Area in the world. However, as we waded in the water I playfully knocked her down in two feet of water and she reacted as if she was drowning. That was the end of the ocean for her. She spent the remainder of her time stretched out by the pool and that was it. At night we went to the local spot, "the Jankaroo," and also to the Casino where we met Angela Davis—the radical freedom fighter from Los Angeles.

At the end of our stay and on our last day, at Paradise Island, President Tisch sent a bottle of scotch to our room. Since I was a teatotaler, I gave it to the maid. After four days and three nights, we flew to Orlando, Florida where Disney World just opened. I thought it was going to be a juvenile experience, but it turned out to be more than I expected. It was actually lots of fun. After our honeymoon, we returned to Minnie's home and prepared for our journey to New York and our new parish. We initially moved into temporary quarters larger than my apartment, while the parsonage was being repaired for us at Fish Avenue in the Bronx. I began pastoring at St. John's on the first Sunday in August in 1972.

The World Is My Parish

Thinking back, after I left the pastorate in Ahoskie, I felt moved by the vision of John Wesley, when a local circuit preacher of his day asked him. "Where was his parish?" To this Wesley replied, "The world is my parish." I felt that I had grown out of my pastorate in Ahoskie and it was time for me to go.

I experimented with the idea of leaving earlier than I did, when I was called to the Garfield Park Baptist Church in Chicago. They even offered me a lucrative package to become Co-Pastor to the Reverend Bob O'Dean, which was double the package I had in Ahoskie. The offer included:

- $12,000 when I was making $7,000;
- M & M Insurance, when I had my own in Ahoskie;
- The full package of an American Baptist pastor.

When I received that call, I immediately called my Board of Deacons and shared with them that I was called to Chicago and questioned if they felt my ministry was finished at Ahoskie Baptist? Each one said that he felt there was more for me to do.

I felt above and beyond the priestly functions of the pastorate; I enjoyed:

- The services of Baptism;
- Doing weddings;
- Caring for the bereaved; and most of all,
- Preaching the Word of God.

Yet, I felt driven to a calling to the wider world, no longer just to the local parish duties within the sacred walls of the edifice.

The deacons prayed with me and asked me to stay. After fasting, praying and holding out for a month, I informed the people at Garfield Baptist Church in Chicago, that I would not be able to accept their call. I thanked them for the opportunity and added that I was not sure it was the move for me at that time.

In May, 1969, I received an invitation from Bill Jones my ever present schoolmate, to be the executive Secretary of S.C.L.C. Operation Breadbasket in New York. After much prayer. again, I infuriated my dear friend by informing him that I didn't feel driven to be the Executive Secretary of Operation Breadbasket of Greater New York at that time.

Needless to say, after turning down both calls I drifted for the remaining months of the year and felt completely driven by the Holy Spirit that, if the call ever came again, I would have to go.

Must Needs Move

A preacher comes to a point in time when he feels an *inner call* to move on. I felt driven that if ever the call came again, I would have to go because I became consumed with the passion that the world was my parish.

So when Jones made me the same offer five months later in August, 1969, I knew in my heart of hearts that my time had come to go—that it was time for me to leave. I enjoyed the years at Ahoskie. They were idyllic years. I came to them as a seminarian student at the age of twenty-five and was a complete novice. When it came to pastoring, never at any time did they attempt to diminish or belittle me. New Ahoskie Church was a dream pastorate, with a congregation of 250, in the heart of a small town of 7,000 people. It was the leading Black church in the Choanoke area that made up four counties. The church had twenty two school teachers and the only guidance counselor in the entire county. H.D. Cooper was the principal of the largest school in Hertford County. He had worked on his Ph.D. at Columbia University in New York. New Ahoskie was a thriving congregation that provided leadership in the Association, State Convention and the Lott Cory Missionary Baptist Foreign Mission Convention. I was blessed with all of that and at the end of seven years, I felt it was time to go.

In Breadbasket, I discovered my *true calling.* Although, the world became my parish, my heart hungered for the local parish, for an anchoring not a drifting from mission to mission without a local anchor.

So, when I received the call to re-enter the local parish, again I felt that I had used up my usefulness being an executive of a Metropolitan Civil Rights Organization.

I must say that Breadbasket opened me up to the idea of God not only being a God of love and mercy, but most of all, to the other side of love which is justice from the Abrahamic motif, which queried the almighty when Abraham asked, "Will not the God of all the earth do just?"

Traveling Full Circle

I had come full circle to have entered back into the pastorate of St. John's. Although the *income* was meager, I saw a calling of God upon my life, where I felt that I would not be smothered if I stayed at Immanuel to fly with unrestricted barriers of race and class.

It was quite a venture to be back in the pastorate in New York. After growing up in North Carolina, New York was the *Sodom and Gomorrah* of the world, as it was portrayed in the media as drug, crime infested, cold and unfriendly, and according to many, I wasn't going to make it. So it was with some trepidation that I entered the pastorate of all places in Harlem, New York.

Harlem, New York

The welcomes were warm when I arrived in Harlem. To my surprise, the Harlem that I embraced consisted of parishioners who were originally from the south, the Caribbean and scattered states between Virginia and Florida. They were just as warm in Harlem, as avid southern church goers. Yet, as a stranger it can be quite anxiety rising, to socialize and familiarize yourself with those at the top, when you feel you are at the bottom of the ladder and just beginning.

The officers offered to furnish the personage but I chose to buy my own furniture and to *sleep in my own bed*. My thinking was that if I got put out into the street so to speak, at least I would have my own bed.

As I didn't have the money to furnish my house, Mr. Wilbur Levine, the President of Martin's Department Store in Brooklyn, offered that if I ever needed him I should feel free to call. And so I did. He gave me the hook-up to A& S Department Store and I was grateful, although I paid the debt off slowly myself.

It was quite a move for my wife to leave her warm, cozy hometown of Portsmouth, Virginia which was part of Tidewater, and go to a city of complete strangers. However, everyone was very gracious to her as we settled in.

Alice White, former wife of Reverend John White of Philadelphia, gave a welcome reception for Minnie. Those in attendance were Mrs. Cynthea Ray, wife of Dr. Sandy Ray, President of Empire Baptist State Convention and Mrs. Nan James, wife of Reverend Hilton James Pastor of Berean Baptist Church in Brooklyn. With faith in God, I believed I could make it. I felt this way although my mentor Reverend Dr. J. Pius Barbour from Crozer was given to the stereotype that one couldn't last one year in Harlem. He said these words to Dr. Proctor, Reverends Jones and Carter when we all gathered in 1965 at the Sheraton in Philadelphia where Dr. King was honored.

Dr. Barbour

Dr. King was mentored by Dr. Barbour when he was a student at Crozer and King was influenced by Barbour to pursue his Ph.D. Degree at Boston University. Dr. King was a frequent visitor in Barbour's parlor where he hammered out his ideas of theological nonviolence. However, King was unable to honor Barbour because he was in Grenada, Mississippi when someone took a shot at James Meredith. Meredith was the first Black person to integrate the University of Mississippi, or Ole Miss as it was called. As a result of the shooting incident, Dr. King couldn't make it, but we proceeded to honor Dr. Barbour anyway. I can't ever forget that Dr. Barbour was the first Black to graduate from Crozer Seminary on a bet to the president that if he didn't get A's, Crozer could remain segregated. It can be said today, that Dr. Barbour is responsible for breaking the color line at Crozer. We had a great night in Philadelphia, but I will never forget Barbour's words about not being able to last more than a year in Harlem. Ironically, Dr. Proctor and I ended up eventually pastoring in Harlem. Proctor pastored at Abyssinian until his retirement and I am still standing. It was during this time that Stokley Carmichael interjected his idea of Black power and the idea took off.

Grief

When I arrived at St. John's, I wasn't aware of the shocking death of Reverend Walter T.C.J. Willoughby, my predecessor. He was found dead in his bed on Sunday New Year's Day in 1971. While his congregation waited for him to arrive for service, someone went to his residence and found him dead. His sudden death almost destroyed the congregation and the deacons were torn and in conflict over him. Reverend Willoughby was quite an orator, tremendous singer and revivalist and was well loved by the community.

When I met with the Board, I ran into those conflicting, unresolved feelings that they had for Reverend Willoughby. I knew then that I had to walk softly, gain their trust, and try to spiritually build back the congregation. I turned to Reverend William Garrison, the Associate, who was an older man and had also been a candidate for the pastor's position. He was very gracious and respectful and counseled me spiritually. Although he was in his eighties, he was very vibrant and no nonsense.

Deacon Richard Crenshaw, Chairman of the Board of Christian Education, was quite a God-fearing person, family man and leader in the community. He was progressive, community minded and the greatest servant of God and the community I have ever met. With his assistance, my first effort was to have a Board of Christian Education Retreat at our Baptist Camp in Pouquay, which turned out to be a huge success. We took a representative group from the various boards and ministers of the church, and we focused on youth ministry and outreach in the spirit of evangelism.

St. John's Community Center

The St. John's Community Center was built in 1970 by Reverend Willoughby, the former pastor and named in honor of the first pastor Dr. Wilson Major Morris. Building the center became possible by obtaining a loan from Herbert Greene, President of Carver Bank on 125th Street.

We had a heavy monthly mortgage that was financed by the bank in addition to our monthly operating expenses of the ministry of St. John's. I was asked by Mrs. Elizabeth McMillan, the Secretary of the Trustee Board to hold off cashing my paycheck on several occasions due to the shortage of funds. My check was my only source of income. At the same time, I was paying my wife's tuition as she was in her senior year at Norfolk State University in Norfolk, Virginia. It was a test of faith, but we managed.

One of the first difficulties I ran into was the Summer Youth Program, in the Community Center. A group of boys ganged up on Quail Johnson, the Director and broke his arm. I was asked to step in and try to help resolve the conflict. Surprisingly, it was easily resolved. The Summer Youth Program was funded by the Police Athletic League (P.A.L.) through the 30th Precinct on 152nd Street and Amsterdam Avenue. Although the Center was productive with the use of the Summer Youth Program during the summer months, the building remained empty during the winter.

Installation

Interestingly, I was not installed as pastor in the same month I arrived. My installation was held in October 1972. Reverend M. L. Wilson, Senior Pastor of Convent Avenue Baptist Church (and a frequent speaker for President Richard Nixon at the White House Chapel), conducted my installation in conjunction with the Baptist Ministers Conference of Greater New York. It was both interfaith and inter-racial. And the white pastor of the North Presbyterian Church, as well as the white rector of the Chapel of the Intercession Episcopal Church turned out to be warm brothers. My dear friend and Crozer schoolmate, the Reverend Ben Whipper was also present; he pastored the Southern Baptist Church, at 108th Street and Central Park West. Concerning all the hoopla and disturbance regarding the former pastor, I thought it best to be installed as quickly as possible, so that there would be no question as to whether I was pastor or not.

The Percentage Giving Program

Reporting on the money raised in the church, was done every 4th Sunday with groups lined up against the wall, reciting what was raised for the month. I resolved to have a more sacred and biblical way of raising money for the church. So I introduced the "Percentage Giving Program," where everyone would no longer be able to be a member in good and regular standing by giving only a quarter a Sunday, equal to $12.00 per year.

First, I proposed, and the church voted that we do away with *dues paying cards*, and that we institute "every member every Sunday giving" of his/her tithes and offerings.

Second, with the Percentage Giving Program we did a survey of the needs of the church, conducted by brother, Robert White, a social worker from the Department of Social Service: We listed:

- Our immediate needs;
- Our short term and long term goals

George Wilkinson was the facilitator. Brother White wrote up our findings and presented them at our "Evening Dinner in our Fellowship Hall" in the lower auditorium. It was adopted by the church. One of the most powerful trustees got up and spoke against it saying, "All he wants is money, when we need to be saving souls." He was correct, but at the same time we had to operate the church on a Biblical and ministry needs basis, with each believer giving as the Lord blessed him/her to give. This statement by the stately brother intimidated me with the fear of being charged with "the intimidating charge of always begging for money," without my understanding then as I do now, that "worship" is:

- Giving yourself in service to God;
- Giving of your tithes and talents unto God; and
- Giving of your materials, financial means as to how the Lord has blessed you!

I regret to this day, that I did not see deeper into the whole spiritual concept of giving as I do now. There is no longer any fear but faith in the whole concept of discipleship and stewardship of "self-surrender" unto God of one's total life. God only asked us to "return His portion" (the tithe), as well as our own gifts in offering unto Him. Hallelujah!

The After School Youth Program

I met the Reverend Bernard Holiday in our Breadbasket Retreat in the previous year at Greenwich, Connecticut. Bernard was the Director of the Manhattan Division of the New York City Council of Churches. I was aware that they were seeking to open a youth program in the churches of Harlem and I called and set up a meeting with our officers. I was filled with fear and trepidation, because they didn't want to use the Wilson Major Morris Community Center for anything but luncheons, plays and dinners for St. John's members. The "Official Board" of Deacons and Trustees approved of the program and the center was opened for the first time from Monday through Friday, 4:00 P.M. to 7:00 P.M., with a male and female director for the young people of the community.

However, the Centre floundered for several years without an outreach program during the day until June, 1977.

The Nutrition Program

The youth program, through the Council of Churches, ended in spring, 1977 for the lack of funds. The Council of Churches ran into financial hard times and therefore the youth program could not sustain itself. We were still burdened with the mortgage note, along with a high Con Edison Bill each month on top of the operating ministry of St. John's Church.

The P.A.L. Program for the summer, 1976 was also cut back. Through Mrs. Gwen Crenshaw, Founder and Director of the Discovery Room for Children (which was a day care program), our Summer Youth Program from the federal government was sponsored.

In April, 1977 I heard through Mrs. Gwen Jones, Director of Harlem Teams and Mrs. Katie Hicks of Abyssinian Baptist Church, that the Department for the Aging was looking for other sponsors in the Harlem Community. She proposed St. John's Community Center, since it sat empty during the week and because there were no other "nutrition programs" for seniors between 145th and 156th Streets. The Hamilton Grange program headed by Reverend M. L. Wilson, Pastor of Convent Avenue Baptist Church, was located on 145th Street and Convent Avenue and the Bethune Center headed by Mr. West was located on 156th Street and St. Nicholas Avenue. Seniors had to climb up steep hills to access each Center. St. John's located on West 152nd Street between Amsterdam and Convent Avenues was the most accessible location. We therefore, pursued our inquiry of sponsorship for a senior program.

Inter-Agency Council

Gwen Jones was also the president of Inter Agency Council of Senior Centers in Harlem and she along with Mrs. Katie Hicks pushed fervently for St. John's.

I was contacted by the Department for the Aging (D.F.T.A.) and met them along with Mrs. Gwen Crenshaw of our church, who also headed her own program Discovery Room for Children. We met with Mrs. Gerry Wooten, the Program Officer, Department for the Aging who was rather dubious about our funding.

Mrs. Crenshaw and I met with Mrs. Wooten a second time, and this time Mrs. Crenshaw knew one of the elected officials from our district. We took her into the meeting, whereupon Gerry Wooten exclaimed, "Oh, I see you've become politically smart like everyone else."

Under Mrs. Wooten's supervision, although we were chosen and sponsored by the Harlem Meals on Wheels, I called our joint Official Board together and informed them of the Department's decision.

There was much opposition because the head officers of St. John's were opposed to our opening up the Center to a senior program. Some said we were giving the Center away. I reminded one of the good brothers that he said Reverend Jackson, Pastor of Church on the Hill had his program on 156th Street and St. Nicholas Avenue, the Reverend Wilson had his program at Convent Avenue Baptist Church, and St. John's had nothing. I added, "Thank you, St. John's now has theirs."

From the beginning, that brother head officer of St. John's always operated at a distance, and never sought to counsel me in having the best outreach possible through our center. Nevertheless, I formed a Board of Directors of which I was the Chair and Mrs. Crenshaw was the Vice Chair. We also formed a Personnel Committee, a Nutrition Committee and a Senior Advisory Board. Mrs. Crenshaw was also a School Board Member in our School District 6.

Wilson Major Morris Center Opening

The Center opened on June 20, 1977. The Center was flooded daily with with over 120 seniors although we were only funded for 110. We did so well that by September, the Department for the Aging spun us off as our own sponsor. It was a great day and members of the church— Deacon Edward Smith, Earlen Glenn, Florine Wyche and others got jobs.

The Department added two other programs under our sponsorship— Drew Hamilton and Annunciation Roman Catholic Church. We were aided by two persons daily from our church, Ms. Ruby Duncan, the Treasurer from Fidelis Federal Credit Union, and Mrs. Gladys Young, the Head of the Credit Committee of Fidelis. They monitored the Center daily, without compensation or any remuneration.

The Center was customized in accordance with the guidelines of the City and became one of the largest outreach multi services of any religious organizations in the city, with over 42 full time workers, 2 vans and 5 nutrition centers in the history of New York.

The New Kitchen

Somewhere in 1978 the city decided to expand our kitchen in order that a larger number of meals could be served, and so that they could supply meals to Canaan Baptist Church's Nutrition Program on 116th Street and to Church of the Master and staff on Morningside Avenue and 123rd Street.

They proposed three suggestions:

- Extending the existing kitchen onto the gymnasium floor;
- Moving the kitchen to the second floor of the Center; or
- Having the meals prepared across the street in St. John's Kitchen, and have the meals transferred across the street on a daily basis.

Opposition was brewing and for resolution purposes a meeting was held that night.

Eureka!

Deacon Alexander McMillan saw me the day of the meeting and asked, "Don't we have land behind the Center, about 100 feet deep and 80 feet wide? When I replied, "Yes." Deacon McMillan replied, "Then why can't we build in the back instead?" Our architect Mr. Legendre said, "Wow! It was a perfect idea." The money that the City was giving was inadequate, and some on the board felt we should forget it; but the idea came up that we could raise the rest.

State Assemblyman Denny Farrell chaired our fund raising committee for which we organized three categories of donors:

- $500 and above—Benefactors
- $250 and above—Patrons
- $100 and above—Donors

It was a joy to see the members of St. John's dig in and raise the remainder of the money.

After the fundraiser the remaining balance of $40,000 was raised.

The late Congressman Ted Weiss broke ground, along with the late City Councilman Stanley Michaels and the other Board members. Following the opening ceremony, we began supplying food to Canaan Baptist and Church of the Master.

Youth Employment

Mrs. Gwen Crenshaw learned that the Department of Labor "Youth Employment Training Program (Y.E.T.P.) was receiving proposals. We met at Ruby Duncan's home and finished a proposal at 2:00 A.M. Mrs. Crenshaw put the "finishing touches" to the proposal which she and I submitted five minutes before the deadline.

- We had 80 Summer Y.E.T.P. youth and 40 after school positions;
- GED training in the lower auditorium at St. John's;
- Office and clerical skills on the second floor of the center in the Walter C.T.J. Willoughby Room;
- Food service management in our new kitchen;
- A Job Placement Officer who got jobs for the trainees;
- Jobs at the Waldorf Astoria in food management
- Enrolled the youth in colleges and the armed forces.

It was indeed a great joy to serve the youth of our community and there were over 30 work sites that accepted our youth for the summer.

Housing

The winter of 1978 was the worst snow storm in New York in eighty years, and as I stood at my window of the parsonage on Fish Avenue in the Bronx; I could hear the aches and groans of the seniors in 450-452 West 152nd Street located next door to the church. Sister Lee was an old lady of the church and ninety years old. She had heat and hot water in her building only two days during the winter. As I stood at my window looking out on the snow, I heard the voice of God say to me, "How dare you sit here in your home with heat and hot water when the people next door to the church don't have either. I am the same God that took you up, and can take you down. How dare you!" I replied. "Lord I'll try."

Working with H.P.D.

I got a sign and put it up in Sister Lee's building at 450-452 West 152nd Street.

The sign invited tenants to a meeting in our Center in order to organize for heat and hot water. Mr. Lowe, a school teacher and Mr. Japeth Banks who tried earlier to organize the tenants, failed to do so and became discouraged.

When the head officers of St. John's saw the sign, he asked me in rebuking tones, "Where do you think you're going with that sign. If I was you, I wouldn't be bothered with them N------!" To this I replied, "And yes, when the squatters take over the building and we try to get them out, those same N------ will burn down this church!" To say the least, it was like raising the dead to get the tenants to come out to a meeting concerning their own welfare. At the third meeting, a Mr. Burke who lived in 450 said that he would put the "Letter of Intent" under each door to get at least 60% of the tenants to sign.

I gave H.P.D. ten people who would work with the tenants in organizing and managing their building. Deacon John Shipp was chosen as the Administrator. He did the following:

- Got the rents up to date;
- Stabilized the rent Got insurance on the building;

- Got a new boiler installed;
- Got a new locked door installed for the entrance

We turned 450 through 452 around. It was nearly an abandoned building with vacant, deteriorating apartments. If we hadn't stepped in, H.P.D. would not have been involved anymore.

American Baptist Church Metro Assistance

Reverend Don Marlon, the Associate Secretary of American Baptist Church (A.B.C. Metro) gave us a lot of housing assistance and guidance. Don also had St. John's written up in the A.B.C. Nationwide Magazine, telling the story of how one church led the tenants on their block to organize and manage their own building. We later helped 464 West 152nd Street, 824 St. Nicholas Avenue on 151st Street, including the Project Basement on 153rd Street between Amsterdam and Broadway to become cooperatives.

Housing Preservation Development's History (H.C.C.I)

In the early 1980s Reverend David Licoish, who was a former assistant pastor to the late Rev. Adam Clayton Powell, Jr. paid an important visit to my office at St. John's Baptist Church. During his visit he shared with me that there were three buildings for sale in the vicinity of 153 and 154th Street. The buildings were attached, three story buildings on St. Nicholas Avenue between 153 and 154th Street which he thought St. John's might be interested in purchasing,

Well, I wasn't interested in St. John's owning rental property as a way of acquiring additional monies for church operation when I believed in Tithing and the principle of Christian Stewardship as the means of underwriting the church ministries. He was persistent about the idea of the church playing a role in acquiring abandoned property; he asked me if I would meet with the head of Housing Preservation and Development (HCCI), at Our Souls Episcopal Church located on the corner of 115th Street and St. Nicholas Avenue.

I agreed to meet with the rector of the church in the Fellowship Hall of the church. We discussed further ideas of an expanding role that churches could play in acquiring properties as a way of providing needed housing for the Harlem community which was a scourged and blighted area of abandoned buildings. As the discussion continued, the idea of the Nehemiah Housing Project in East New York Brooklyn "hit me." The Nehemiah Housing Project was headed by Rev. Dr. Johnny Ray Youngblood, the pastor of St. Paul's Baptist Church in East New York. Youngblood had organized the Black churches in East New York to enter into a coalition with the Catholic Diocese of Brooklyn and Long Island, to provide better and suitable housing for people of that area. He had an Industrial Area Foundation (I.A.F.) which was founded by the late Saul Alinsky in Rochester, New York to come and give ongoing training skills to the ministers. By doing this, Youngblood captured the attention of the leaders of Brooklyn, New York, including Mayor Koch whose interest was in the housing work that was done for several blocks in the East New York area.

I spoke to the group as to whether they could build upon the work Rev. Youngblood had done and suggested that I have them meet with my group and share the work they accomplished with the churches in East New York.

I knew Rev. Youngblood personally because we both previously worked as the Assistant Pastor to Rev. Bill Jones. I liked their interest and invited Youngblood to speak at the next meeting. He couldn't attend but sent Rev. Clarence Williams who was the Pastor of the Southern Baptist Church on Rockaway Avenue, in East New York. He came and related the story of the Nehemiah Housing Project.

As the meeting got underway, we thought of Rev. John J. Sass as a pastor to talk to since he had built the new edifice of St. Matthew's Baptist Church, on the corner of Macomb's Place and 150th Street. Rev. John Sass talked to Dave Licoish and invited the ministries to meet at his fellowship hall. We had a meal prepared to serve the fifteen clergy persons who came. Among them were: the Rev. Dr. Wyatt Tee Walker, who had already supervised the erecting of several buildings in Harlem. Rev. Preston R. Washington piggybacked on the work that St. John's had done in organizing tenants, in *abandoned* buildings across the street from Memorial Baptist Church.

The Rev. Bishop Norman Quick, Pastor of Child's Memorial Church of God in Christ and friend of Dr. Walker, The Rev. Patricia Rheburg, of the Council of Churches including the Rev. Dr. James Forbes, Pastor of Riverside Church, in New York and others, agreed to invite I.A.T. to Harlem headed by Ed. Chambers. We named our circle Harlem Churches for Community Improvement (H.H.C.I.), but we had to raise $75,000 in order for I.A.F. to come. We embarked on the mission to raise the money and report the monies at Child's Memorial where Bishop Quick invited the group for the next meeting. I went to our church conference and at our conference shared the noble idea of the Pastors. To my shock, the Chairperson of the Trustee Board at the time said he would never agree for St. John's to put money into any project headed by the Pastors of New York because they had never done anything. He went on to say that he would agree to allow me to raise the money from the congregation, I would be free to do so. How wrong Hightower was because all of our churches were founded by *Rebel Pastors*. The motion prevailed and I asked Mrs. Evelyn Bell (President of the Senior Choir) and her husband George Bell to head the effort to raise funds from the members. They did a good job of collecting over $250.00 along with other churches reporting like at Child's Memorial.

We (the Pastors) fell short of our goal of $75,000 whereupon the late Rev. Canon Frederick Boyd Williams said, "He thought he could appeal to the Episcopal Diocese of New York, because he had personal contact with Bishop Paul Moore of the Diocese." Bishop Moore put up the remainder and I.A.F. came in and did their first organizing training at St. Mark's Methodist Church on St. Nicholas Avenue and 136th Street, where Rev. John Smith was the pastor.

Deacons John Shipp and Edward Smith of St. John's volunteered to be the trainees from the church. H.C.C.I., elected Rev. Dr. Preston R. Washington as its first President; Rev. Dr. Wyatt Tee Walker as Vice President; and the Rev. Norman Quick as the Treasurer. H. C. C. I. inspired and initiated the total housing *renaissance* in Harlem.

Twenty-five years later, H.C.C.I. has built over fifteen buildings of 6,500 units; and an H.I.V. AIDS Program and multiple services to the community. It is the largest housing complex in the nation headed by a consortium of Pastors.

The Rev. Clarence Grant came up with the idea that if Central Harlem could put forth such a humongous effort, couldn't we organize in West Harlem and do the same.

We met at First Calvary Baptist Church where Rev. Richard Watkins was the Pastor and organized the West Harlem Churches Cluster of Churches. Rev. S. Frank Emmanuel, Pastor of St. Luke, A.M.E., was the President; Rev. Grant, was the Vice President and the Rev. Robert Johnson was staff assistant to Rev. Grant. We got the initiative off the ground in a grand way like we had done with H.C.C. I had several meetings at Macedonia Baptist Church where Rev. Isaac Graham was the pastor. Rev. Grant got Planning Board #9 to support our effort to build a forty apartment unit on West 138th Street between Hamilton Place and Broadway. Unfortunately we had already been outbid by an organization that was already involved in housing.

In the meantime, West Harlem Cluster of Churches, Inc., was asked to sponsor The Bethune Senior Citizens Nutrition Program located on the corner of Amsterdam Avenue and 157th Street. It provided breakfast, lunch and dinner to one hundred and ten seniors. The late Canon Williams, was the Chairman of the Personal Committee and I was his Vice Chair and eventually became Chairman of the Board, as well as of the Personnel Committee.

CHAPTER THIRTEEN

THE DRUG EPIDEMIC

Ossie Davis/Rev. Wendell Foster

Around the time as all the housing issues were taking place, Rose Ward, Head of 145th Street Day Care Center and I went to the 30th Precinct to ask that Captain Seymour do something about the increasing drug problem. Seymour's reply was that he wasn't going to follow in the shoes of his predecessor Captain Casey.

Captain Casey had met earlier with Farther Nolan, of St. Catherine Catholic Church, Mr. Bloomberg and I, in the fellowship room of St. Catherine's Roman Catholic Church around the terrible sites of drug trafficking. Casey helped us by trying to keep the drug trafficking under control. We met on a monthly basis, until Captain Casey was moved to the Bronx, as a disciplinary action, because he allegedly acted on his own without his supervisor's consent. However, the meetings were later moved to the Bronx.

Casey joined Rev. Wendell Foster, Actor Ossie Davis and I as we called on all churches to keep their doors open in a 24 hour prayer vigil in order to rid the area of the increasing drug trafficking. We met with Commissioner Ben Ward regarding the rising drug problem and he instituted the first "Drug Hotline" in the city for the public.

When we were rejected by Captain Seymour of the 30th Precinct, we were stalled and appalled at the same time. Some of the police officers who knew me asked if we would do something. I answered yes, and contacted the National Public Radio regarding the drug problems in our community.

National Public Radio

I went on national radio describing the growing drug problem in the New York are and took the reporter to the various sites that I knew were operating in full view of the Police Department. The British Broadcasting Network contacted me at that time and did coverage of the area. Reverend Calvin Butts joined me in that interview.

The situation became so bad that two of the clergy in the Harlem community asked me to go with them to the Commissioner to address the problem, but neither of them showed up. So what was I to do?

Well, the Holy Spirit said to me, "You can't cancel the meeting. Let them know that you speak for the community, and that you are not alone. I am with you, with all the Holy Angels of Heaven." With that I went alone into the "Battle Room" of One Police Plaza to see the Commissioner Ben Ward. The Commissioner asked me what did I want. I told him that I wanted him to come to our community and address the people regarding the terrorizing problem they were living with day and night, as the shooting all through the night was like a war torn area. He agreed and met in a community meeting in our Wilson Major Morris Community Center, and took questions from the floor regarding the drug problem in our area.

Hearing on Police Brutality

Commissioner Ward was the first African-American Commissioner in the City of New York. We held a massive meeting at the 169th Street Armory which led to the selection of the first African-American Police Commissioner, for the City of New York. The meeting was led by Reverend Calvin Butts and Jesse Jackson was the keynote speaker. When Jesse Jackson entered the armory, a chorus of chants rang out, "Run, Jesse run!" The crowd was referring to the 1984 presidential election.

Commissioner Ward was responsive to our cry and working alongside him was Mr. Calvin Solomon, the NYC District Attorney's Officer for Community Affairs.

At the same time, a terrible drug problem was occurring on St. Nicholas Place near 155th Street. The lobby of 79 St. Nicholas Place was occupied by drug pushers and users, and District Attorney Calvin Solomon and I had been meeting with several tenants. We came up with the idea of trying to put up a "No Trespassing" sign in the lobby. It worked so well that it became a plan that now covers the entire city, and this began at 79 St. Nicholas Place, thanks to the persistent help of Calvin Solomon.

Following Commissioner Ward, Lee Brown became the second African-American Police Commissioner. Upon his appointment, he held an introductory meeting at the American Red Cross Building on Amsterdam Avenue and 66th Street. In the meeting he asked the churches, temples and synagogues to "adopt a block" from a crime infested area.

Adopt-A-Block

St. John's became the first church in the city to "Adopt-A-Block", and the block was St. Nicholas Place between 152nd and 155th Street.

As the pastor, I decided to have monthly meetings with the tenants and the new Police Captain. The area was so bad, that the tenants asked that I not state the actual reason for the monthly meetings in the flyers that we passed out. The residents told their scared neighbors that they were going to monthly choir rehearsal meetings.

The "Adopt-A-Block" idea continued for a while and we met in other areas, sharing with them how the Captain and the pastor of a church jointly sponsored the monthly meetings of the Adopt-a-Block Program.

The Dirty Thirty

The 30th Precinct is the designated precinct for the church community in the vicinity of 152 Street. When I arrived at St. John's Church, the 30th Precinct was one of the highest crime ridden facilities of Harlem in

Manhattan, and St. John's was located down the block. Cops were found guilty of stealing cash, guns and drugs. It was the worst time during the history of the New York's Police Department. Due to the internal corruption, the precinct earned the nickname the *Dirty 30.*

When Commissioner Bratton arrived in New York during the Giuliani Administration, he immediately and vigorously investigated the "War on Drugs". Officers of the 30th Precinct were found guilty of collusion with drug "Kingpins" in the area. Bratton went personally to the 30th Precinct and lifted the police badges off the guilty officers. The news shook up the Police Department at its core. I developed tremendous respect for Bratton, because he came out into the community. He saw that I along with other church officers were interviewed concerning the notorious drug problem in Central and West Harlem on the Upper West Side.

The 30th Precinct Community Council

At this time, Ms. Hazel O. Reilly, who was the president, held a tremendous Town Hall meeting in the Fellowship Hall of the Chapel of the Crucifixion (the Episcopal Church) with all the major networks present. It was a very scary time because the whole area was terrorized by drug dealers, like maggots over rotten meat.

In his restructuring of the 30th Precinct, Commissioner Bratton appointed Captain Sweeney as the new captain. He also put flood lights at both ends of the 500 hundred block of 152 Street and turned it into a model block.

Harlem Initiative Together (H.I.T.)

Reverend Wyatt Tee Walker, Father Earl Koopercamp, Father Thomas Fenlon of Our Lady of Lourdes Roman Catholic Church and other clergy formed H.I.T. in order to confront the drug problem. They met regularly with Police Commissioner Bratton to get the Initiative moving forward.

Bratton and I happened to be attending a citywide awards ceremony when we met for the first time. We hit it off immediately and in our conversation, I informed him of the rally against drugs being held at the Church of the Intercession. I said it would help to restore *good faith* back to the community, if he would make an appearance at one of the meetings scheduled at 155th Street and Broadway. Bratton came and apologized to the community for the criminal activities of the few at the 30th Precinct. About this time, Reverend Wyatt Walker of Canaan Baptist Church, in Harlem, Father Thomas Fenlon, Rector of Our Lady of Lords Roman Catholic Church, Father Earl Koopercamp, Outreach Minister of Chapel of the Intercession and other clergy also met with Commissioner Bratton.

Reverend Earl Koopercamp

It must be said that Rev. Koopercamp was one of the bravest clergymen at that time because parishioners placed their offering in the worship basket, at the same time he had them drop in the addresses where drugs were being sold. As news media filmed the "spots" being identified, it was obvious that he was among all those who put their lives on the line as they collectively tried to bring down the drug activity. As a result, Father Koopercamp's apartment was burglarized and burned. Yet he remained vigilant in his effort to rid the drug traffic problem.

Father Thomas Felon

Father Thomas Felon, Priest of Our Lady of Lords Roman Catholic Church, went so far in his one man war on drugs as to hold his "Good Friday" service outside. He did this on 139th Street between Hamilton Place and Broadway, which was known as one of the worst drug blocks in the nation.

I joined him in his outdoor Good Friday Service in bringing one of the "Seven Words" of Jesus from the Cross. The street was jammed and packed with drug dealers and users. I probably felt as scared as Dr. King did when he met in Philadelphia, Mississippi after the killing of the three civil rights workers: Schwerner, Chaney and Goodman.

Clergy Coalition on Community Policing (C.C.O.P.)

Reverend Koopercamp called a meeting of the elected officials, community leaders and concerned citizens in the Fellowship Hall of the Church of the intercession. He was elected Chair and I, Co-Chair. We met monthly and organized all of the fourteen beats that covered the 30th Precinct area, from 132nd Street to 155th Street.

Police Officers Rios and Ella Owens helped the leaders immensely, taking sensitive information, never revealing the sources. This was the plan

- Meet on each of the 14 beats;
- Have the residents elect a coordinator for each "beat;"
- Have two officers assigned to each beat.

An annual meeting of The West Side was held in the auditorium of Public School 153 on Amsterdam Avenue and 146th Street. Commissioner Safer who succeeded Bratton was the keynote speaker. Reverend Clarence Grant, pastor of Convent Avenue Baptist Church gave the benediction and opening prayer, and it was good to have him on board.

I was called the "Drug Czar" of Harlem by him and others. I refuted this outright, because there were fifty-five major Columbian and Dominican drug lords who controlled the area.

Reverend Norman Quick/Councilman Stanley Michaels

When the problem got out of control I determined that I was not going to die for not having done anything by a stray or an intended bullet. So I went to my good friend Bishop Norman Quick of Child's Memorial Church of God in Christ, who had no faith in the police. Nevertheless, he said that he would go with me to Councilman Stanley Michaels Office to seek assistance. Stan Michaels helped in many ways. First by sending out the notices for our monthly meetings; second, by having his staff persons, Julio Baptista and Steven Simon, chief of staff present when he was unable to attend. Julio now works for Columbia

Presbyterian Hospital and Steve for the New York City Department of
Parks and Recreation.

White House Citation

Our work was so impressive that it caught the attention of President
Clinton and the White House. We were cited as one of the ways churches
and the police could work together, for the benefit of the community in
which we both served.

CHAPTER FOURTEEN

LIFE AT THE PARSONAGE

Drug Proliferation

Living in St. John's parsonage on Fish Avenue in the East Bronx went well for the first few years. The parsonage is the only undetached house on the block; the remaining houses are two family attached homes. When I moved there in 1972, next door was a plumbing shop that soon closed and remained vacant for a couple of years. Then, a gentleman whom I later met, said that he was opening a record shop, which didn't make sense as it was located three buildings from the corner on a residential, homeowners' street.

To my horror, I noticed white teenagers beginning to congregate in the afternoon following school at the "alleged" record shop next door. I had no knowledge of the drug world and went to the President of our Block Association and complained. I stated that marijuana was being sold on our block and that we knew marijuana kills brain cells and does irreparable damage to the brain. He replied, "It's a matter of opinion."

I was shocked and aghast because he was supposed to be guardian of the block, member of "The Fish Bay" Homeowners Association, which comprised of seventeen blocks. Yet, he was indifferent to the invasion of drugs on our block. Little did I know that his daughter was a Rastafarian. Therefore, he saw no need to do anything.

Captain Austin Mulryan

I visited Captain Mendyke, of the 47th Precinct, and informed him of what was happening on my block. He said he wasn't going to do anything and advised me to go and inform Sterling Johnson. Johnson, was the police officer appointed by Mayor Koch to bring down drugs and violence in Midtown Manhattan. I followed this visit up with one to the District Manager of Planning Board 12, and he did absolutely nothing to assist the community.

When Austin Mulryan became Captain, I went by and asked him whether he had children. When he answered, "Yes", I replied, "I have a twelve year old son and you have a twelve year old daughter. Who knows whether they will meet one day and what the outcome will be, so while we can, let's do something about it." To this he replied, "I will do all I can."

He had the drug dealers in the heart of Boston and Fish Avenues arrested, then they moved their operation into a predominantly business area. He held several "Federal Days" attempting to move the drug dealing out of the area, but it continued to escalate to the corner of Boston Road and Fish Avenue. Drug dealers sat on a large mail box and sold drugs in the open daylight at the intersection, and when the light turned red they made a sale.

A group of us held a rally across the street from the same corner where Reverend Nathaniel Tyler Lloyd, Pastor of Trinity Baptist Church was the keynote speaker. North of Boston Road was one of the largest housing complexes in the Eastchester area of the East Bronx, which also began to experience the infiltration of the drug traffic. A drug training program, "Day Top" held several meetings with the tenants and residents in the surrounding area. The manager, Mr. Cornish cooperated and we worked together along with the 47th Precinct to try to keep the drug problem down.

Mrs. Lydia Morales, Reverend Joseph I. Walker, and Deacon J. B. Clarkson joined me in a visit to the precinct. The drug problem was so bad in the building across the street from the 47th Precinct that the Captain feared for our lives and didn't want us to return to the precinct because it was under surveillance by drug dealers. However, Reverend Walker, Deacon Clarkson and I continued to go to the precinct and meet with P.O. Eddie and police woman Thomasina Robinson.

A Clergy Coalition Idea

One day we met in Reverend Walker's home across the street from me. P.O. Robinson said, "We are having problems in other areas and how come you can't come together and fight as one against this problem?" She said she thought that she could find a local church and clergy who would come together, where the police could discuss this problem.

Father Walker of St. Luke Episcopal Church and P.O. Robinson got the site and we asked that Commissioner Benjamin Ward to be our keynote speaker. Commissioner Ward spoke and after the conclusion of his speech, Father Walker stood and raised the question, "Where do we go from here?"

The idea immediately came to us that we should band together as Protestant, Catholic and Jewish clergy to form a Clergy Coalition and that is just what we called ourselves, the Clergy Coalition of the 47th Precinct. The members were:

- Rev. John L. Scott, President, St. John's Baptist Church
- Fr. Sullivan, 1st Vice President, St. Mary's Roman Catholic Church
- Mr. Leonard Rosen, 2nd Vice President, Violet Hill Synagogue
- Rev. J. Perry Wooten, Treasurer, Fish Bay Presbyterian Church; and
- Police Officer Thomasina Robinson, Secretary

We knew that there might be a conflict of interest for Thomasina to be the secretary; yet she continued in that vein and was the driving force to:

1. Sponsor an M.L.K. Birthday Celebration;
2. Hold a National Night Against Crime in August;
3. Give out free turkeys to the homeless who she knew;
4. Meet with the captain monthly; and
5. Hold rallies and marches.

Rally at Evander Childs High School "Athletic Field"

Our largest rally was held in the athletic field of Evander Childs High School, in the Bronx, N.Y., where people brought their flashlights to see and hear the speeches and choirs sing. We deliberately didn't invite Mayor Koch who angered the Black community across the nation when he attacked "Quotas" in a speech he gave in Philadelphia. To our surprise, he flew into the field anyway, in a police helicopter.

Prayer at Drug Spots

About fifteen clergy met monthly and so we decided to march past each "drug site" and have the ministers of that area and his congregation pray for "Healing and Deliverance."

The Clergy Coalition still exists. I served two "stormy" years. Some thought I was too radical; but I only told the truth as I knew it and used my voice for the defenseless and powerless.

The Reverend G. Earl Knight, Pastor of the North Bronx Seventh Day Adventist Church succeeded me. Reverend Samuel Simpson succeeded him and instituted an awards banquet that gave $500.00 to ten young college people nominated by the churches.

Elaine Williams, a retired school principal, worked with us when we distributed turkeys and became familiar with all of our ideas and efforts, and the next thing I knew, she was elected Precinct Community Council President. The first thing she did was take over and sponsor the clergy police breakfast through the precinct council. It was then called the Police Community Breakfast. We were all taken aback, but since she did such a superb job of bringing out all the local leaders and police brass, we decided to let her have her glory.

CHAPTER FIFTEEN

THE UNITED MISSIONARY BAPTIST ASSOCIATION

My Eureka Moment

While I was involved in the community, I continued to maintain my membership in the Baptist Ministers Conference of Greater New York and Vicinity. I rose in the ranks of our association of churches from second place, to first, and then eventually to Moderator in about a twelve year period.

The United Missionary Baptist Association served 152 churches in Manhattan, the Bronx, Westchester and Rockland Counties. I never dreamed of having to care for all the churches like the Apostle Paul. I was ever mindful that I was a *barefoot country boy* from rural Eastern North Carolina, where I once walked behind a mule and a plow. I never dreamed of pastoring in Harlem, or becoming a Moderator. I really felt inadequate for the job, but thanks be to God there was a *glowing missionary*, Sister Lurleen Chesson, wife of Deacon Al Chesson from New Orleans, Louisiana. In her, I confided my sense of inadequacy for the task, and she kept telling me, "Pastor, you can do it. We are behind you and the church will support you."

The thing that really convinced me was a silent conversation that God had with me at an "unguarded moment" saying, "You were born dead, but didn't I bring you back to life?" You were sick at nine years old, never considered to run and play again; didn't I heal your body? You weren't supposed to finish high school; didn't I graduate you with honors? You weren't supposed to go to college, but didn't I make a way for you? You didn't even know of seminary; didn't I bring you through all of that?" To each one I answered, "Yes, Lord," and he said to me, "If I took you from a mule and plow, why would you doubt me now? I will be the wind beneath your wings." With that, my strength was renewed and my resolve was sure that, as God had seen me through in the past, he would see me through as head of all the churches of Metropolitan, New York.

When it came time for my installation, Mrs. Chesson said, "Pastor, sit back, let me handle all the food and don't call my name." They bought all the chickens, fixed the food and served over 500 delegates in our Wilson Major Morris Community Center. And this was done prior to the installation ceremony.

Reverend Samuel Austin, President of the Empire Missionary Baptist State Convention, preached and he was accompanied by Reverend Dr. Earl Moore, who gave the Installation Charge. Reverend Tim Mitchell **of** Ebenezer Baptist Church in Queens and civil rights warrior was present together with many other pastors and delegates. The church was packed upstairs and down, and although St. John's seats 600 upstairs and 100 downstairs many couldn't get in. It was a glorious night!

Financial Shock

Prior to my installation a major fundraiser was held for the 40th year of the Association. The purpose was to give me a solid financial footing to start. Five days later, I received the "dreaded call" that the Association was broke and the $10,000 check we gave to the Marina Del Ray Catering Hall bounced and the Bronx D.A. gave us five days to make good on the check.

I didn't have any money as my three sons were attending college.

John Jr., was at Fordham Law School, here in New York; James Augustine at George Washington University in D.C., and Jerome Scharif was a freshman at Hampton University in Hampton, Virginia. I didn't know what to do when Reverend Isaac B. Graham, second vice moderator called and said, "Reverend Dukes, first vice moderator worked things out for you; all you have to do is sign on the dotted line for he is the one who is advancing the loan to pay off the bounced check and other debts." We met in Albany, New York and I signed the note.

I made Reverend Nelson C. Dukes my financial officer. This way, we could pay off all of our debts, and know that we could take care of all our delegates to our state and national conventions and congresses. It was a maiden voyage, working with Graham and Dukes. I called them my "Dream Team,"

I never dreamed or had the foggiest idea of ever having to care for the Churches of Christ, like the Apostle Paul. It was always a vintage idea, always to be imagined but never lived.

When reading the Bible of the heroes of faith it is so mythological as if something happened once—only a few to be repeated, but never to the extent that if the heroes and heroines of faith achieved. Their efforts seem so supernatural until you never think of doing things in the same way they did. They appear almost, as deity, and yet we are so frail and weak in comparison to their strength and pursuit.

CHAPTER SIXTEEN

The National Evangelism Movement

A Church Mother's Support

In 1995 I heard of an evangelism conference that was being held at the Franklin Hotel in Philadelphia, Pennsylvania. I attended the conference along with Deacon George Wilkinson of our church. It was the most amazing conference I have ever experienced, and it was led by the Reverend Paul Lee, Pastor of Jones Memorial Baptist Church.

Reverend Bill Burwell was the primary teacher with a manual on "making disciples" in his possession. I met with the joint board of our officers in order to bring the "Discipleship Movement" to our church. There was a lot of bickering back and forth until I told them that I was placing my ministry at St. John's with the movement. The only financial obligation was to pay $250.00 per session, to which they eventually agreed.

Ironically, the first night of training by Bill Burwell was the first board meeting of our association, and I was at the Association Board meeting since it was my first meeting. I chaired with all the pastors including all of the auxiliary heads, and officers to deal with the financial solvency of the Association. When I called back to see how the sessions were going, Mrs. Chesson said, "It was a packed house." I in turn shouted, "Glory to God."

I really felt that it was unfair for me to be emerging as the head of the Association and at the same time to have the most dynamic training program that we had in the history of St. John's Church. I felt that I couldn't neglect the overall responsibility of overseeing the life of the African-American Baptist Churches of Metropolitan, New York.

To my surprise, the work of the Association went well. We met quarterly in a different borough, but the annual session was always held in Manhattan due to transportation accessibility. We met all of our indebtedness and the financial responsibilities of our delegates. The seven auxiliaries were:

- The Parent Body officers;
- The Women's Missionary Auxiliary
- The Laymen's League
- The Usher's Auxiliary
- The Nurses Auxiliary
- The Minister's Wives and Widows
- The Sunday School and B.T.U., as well as our Leadership Training School.

I was blessed when my mother visited from the farm in Roanoke Rapids, North Carolina to be our special guest. I was surprised that she was able to come because the first week in October which is our Annual Session was right in the midst of the harvest season for farm life.

Mother and my brother Oscar carried on the tradition of my father by being, "produce farmers." As they supplied the "Farmer's Market" with produce in Roanoke Rapids, this was an important time for them as farmers. However, she came and I was grateful.

Daddy's Death

Daddy died nine years earlier than my mother, on her birthday— February 10, 1987. Although I honored my father, we were never close because in those days parents kept their distance from the children. Yet his death shook my world like I never dreamed.

He died on the day that I was in a meeting at Berkley Hall with Dr. Kenneth Smith and other Crozer graduates of Colgate/Crozer Divinity School, in Rochester, regarding my degree requirements. As I was finishing my D. Min. Degree at Colgate/Crozer, I needed the assistance of Dr. Kenneth Smith my ethics professor to complete my work. Dean Harold of Penn State University was also present. Around noon, as we were finishing lunch, I received a call from my wife that my father had just died. The news was like I was on an airplane that was suddenly shot out of the sky and plummeted to earth. When I returned to the dining table feeling as dead as a corpse, Dr. Smith took a look at me and asked, "John, what happened?" "My father just died," I explained. Whereupon Dr. Smith said to Harold, "You all take him to get his things and get him to the airport." Associate Elton Trublood, the other Crozer clergy who pastored the parish in Sunshine, Maryland, near the banks of the Susquehanna River off of Highway 95 (going south) was also with us. All I know is that I flew from Rochester to Syracuse, and eventually to Norfolk Municipal Airport. Then I drove a rental car home to Roanoke Rapids to our rural community town of Quankey, I met with Oscar, my brother who lived nearby. He was the person who found our father lying on the floor beside his bed. He tried in vain to resuscitate him until our mother said to him, "Bro, there is nothing else you can do. I found him lying beside the bed when I woke up this morning and he was already cold at that time."

My youngest brother Lynn and I stayed with our mother. Although we stayed up until 2:30 A.M., one of the hardest things for me to do was to go to bed that night, and when I did, I just couldn't seem to fall asleep. However, the most difficult thing was the walk down that long hallway to the room opposite my father's room where I entered for bed, until . . . . . .

An Epiphany

A certain calm suddenly seemed to come over me as I audibly heard the words of the 23rd Psalm, . . ."For thou art with me." With those words I no longer felt abandoned and isolated, but in union with the presence of those words.

We joined hands together and with Oscar, standing next to me, we prayed first. Then Lynn, began to pray to the "Great Spirit." I was shocked and felt that he was being disrespectful to our father, since daddy was a Christian, a life-time member of our ancestral church—the Daniel's Chapel Baptist Church, in Enfield, North Carolina. Nevertheless, I did not try to stop him from praying.

The Indian Movement

I knew that in the northern end of Halifax County there were those claiming their Indian ancestry; these people were previously identified as *colored*. I knew that Lynn tried to get mother to identify her Indian ancestry but she said, "I've been colored all my life and I'm not about to change now."

The next night after Daddy's death, Lynn moved into his room with his collection of rocks and without asking mother's permission. Evidently, Lynn relished rocks as a comforting presence, and when he moved into our father's room, the night following Daddy's burial, he loaded up the room with about twenty rocks, of different sizes and hues. I was shocked!

I was appalled because Daddy never did identify as an Indian. Yet, my mother allowed Lynn to stay there with our third brother Emmit until "all hell broke loose."

I always fantasized about the "Scott Brothers" being a model family—a close knit family. When Daddy died, it seemed like the glue that held us together broke, and we became like any other family in conflict that breaks down during the time of death of a mother or father.

Emmit Shoots at Lynn

Disaster struck on the Tuesday following the Easter egg hunt our mother organized for our children which was customary in those days. As I was checking out of the hotel to head back to New York, my mother called and said, "John come out here quickly. Emmit has just shot at Lynn and the sheriff is on his way."

I immediately saw death hovering in the air. I envisioned a white cop coming to arrest a Black male who had just shot at his brother, while the gun was still in his hand. I was embarrassed because I had hidden the unruly conduct of Emmitt and Lynn from my wife, and now it was here in the wide open for the entire world to see.

I left Minnie and our three sons at the motel and raced five miles out onto the farm and home. When I arrived, Emmit was out in the field with the rifle lying on the ground. I was scared because my thinking was that if he shot at Lynn, who was to say he wouldn't shoot at me next. Well he didn't, although he was very angry and protesting that Lynn called him a faggot and emphasized that he wasn't going to take it.

The White Cop

By this time, the white cop drove up and I greeted him by saying, "I 'm Reverend Scott, the oldest brother."

The cop was respectful and picked up the 22" gauge rifle and didn't give it to Emmitt, he gave it to me. As soon as he left, Emmitt demanded that I give back his gun and I refused. Mother ordered me, "Give Emmitt back his rifle" and I returned it to Emmitt. I was stunned but knew that mother always had a way with Emmitt, whereby he usually got his way. This incident ended the myth of the model of the "Scott Brothers!"

The Association's Guest Lecturer

One of the main features of the Annual Session was a lecture series by a guest preacher Granville Steward, Pastor of Mt. Zion Baptist Church in Newark. He was the lecturer for the second and third Annual Sessions.

My first session's lecturer was the Reverend Paul Lee, Pastor of Jones Memorial Church in Philadelphia. He was also the regional coordinator of the National Evangelism Movement headquartered at the Bethany Baptist Church in Los Angeles. Reverend Rosalia Johnson was the Pastor and President.

I arranged for Reverend Lee to speak to about thirty pastors at the Memorial Baptist Church in New York where Reverend Dr. Preston R. Washington was the pastor. I admired him immensely for his extraordinary vision and leadership talents and looked forward to working with him.

My dream was to have the movement implemented in all of our churches by the end of my four year term. Unfortunately, Reverend Lee did not share my vision. For this fourth and final year, my heart's desire was to have my dear friend and beloved brother Reverend Dr. W. A. Jones, as the lecturer. He came, was his usual and masterful self and sort of put the "icing on the cake."

Dream for Untutored Pastors

This term was used by Howard Thurman in his book, *The Luminous Darkness*. As the saying goes, "There is no such thing as being educated and uneducated. All of us have been tutored." It was on my heart since Crozer days that the so-called "Jack Leg Preachers" would be given their "due credit" for starting our churches, some in living rooms, in funeral parlors, or even in hay lofts (as in the days of oppression).

I wanted to begin a learning program for all ministers, to begin where they were in a certificate program, and move out eventually into the academic and seminary setting, whether they pastored two or two thousand members. Each parishioner deserved the best like any other believer in our so-called most established churches.

I shared my dream with another close friend, the Reverend Dr. Allen Paul Weaver, Pastor of Bethesda Baptist Church in New Rochelle. We hammered out a format in my second year as moderator and presented it to Dr. William Howard who was the President of New York Theological Seminary. He liked the idea but said, "I don't mean to limit it to Baptists but a cross section of interested clergy." Dr. Howard decided to call together a summit of regional pastors of about ten to fifteen members, who liked the idea as well.

Clergy Refreshment Program (C.R.P.)

In my effort to get it off the ground, I asked Dr. Howard to give the commencement address to our Leadership Training School at Mt. Carmel Baptist Church in the Bronx. At the time, the Reverend Dr. Anthony Lowe was the pastor and in his third year. To finally force Dr. Howard's hand, I asked him to prepare a brochure to be distributed when he delivered the installation message, at the new Mt. Zion Baptist Church in Manhattan. The Reverend Carl Washington, Jr. was the pastor and this was during my final year. Before we could meet again, Dr. Howard was called as the pastor to the Bethany Baptist Church in Newark, New Jersey. So I saw my C.R.P. Dream just vanish into thin air with Dr. Howard's departure.

My successor was the Reverend Nelson C. Dukes, Pastor of Fountain Spring Baptist Church in the Bronx. Thankfully, one of his first acts was to name the Associate Ministers Division "The Reverend John L. Scott Associate Ministers Division" in my honor.

The Associate Ministers Division

The Associate Ministers Division began during my first year as Moderator, and it was the first time all the licensed and ordained non–pastors were called together to:

- Learn the role of Associate and assistants
- Know their duties

Learn ministerial ethics and to help them prepare for areas of ministerial service and pastoral leadership.

I departed in 2000, having led one of the most miraculous and successful roles of moderator of which one could ever dream.

W. Franklin Richardson

It was also during my moderating that the gifted and charismatic Reverend Dr. W. Franklin Richardson ran for the President of the National Baptist Convention, Inc.,USA. It was our dream that "Rich" would become one of the greatest denominational leaders we would ever see, but due to circumstances that remained a mystery, he didn't make it. However, on the day of voting in Tampa in 2002, the Washington Post had him leading Reverend William Shaw by 4 to 1. Shaw won the presidency by only 300 plus votes out of 60,000 delegates. Richardson on the other hand, went on to become the Chairman of the Board of the National Action Network headed by the Reverend Al Sharpton.

The Social Justice Award

I was honored to be asked by my good friend "Reverend Al" to serve on his national board. We knew each other earlier since we worked together when he was, "Youth Director of Operations Breadbasket" in New York and I was the Executive Secretary. At this annual meeting, Reverend Sharpton always honored those true "Freedom Fighters" and named the "The Social Justice Award," for Reverend Dr. W. A. Jones.

In 2005, I was honored by receiving the W. A. Jones Social Justice Award, along with the Reverend Dr. Fred Shuttlesworth, leader of the Birmingham Movement, and the Reverend Gardner C. Taylor, Dean of Black Preachers in America and former pastor of Concord Baptist Church.

A King Fellow

One of my highest honors came when I was inducted into "the Hall of Fame" as a "King Fellow" of the Martin Luther King, Jr., Chapel of Morehouse College in Atlanta.

A King Fellow was only granted to graduate candidates of African origin for continued study. To qualify, one was required to be a stellar student, who demonstrated high leadership skills, and a proven track record of community service.

The Evangelism/Discipleship Program

I continued to stay involved in the life of St. John's Church as its pastor, because it was only as its pastor that I was free to do some of the things listed in this treatise.

The Evangelism/Discipleship Program was the pulse beat of my heart. It started in 1995, and was meant to be a three year Discipleship Training Program. It eventually engulfed every member of the church, equipping them in ways to share their faith and to win the lost to Christ. It got off the ground in an electrifying way, which became a way of "Lay Take Over" of the church, apart from the established leaders of deacons, trustees and deaconesses.

There were five training sessions going on simultaneously, and each unit had its own teacher. Ideally, no teacher stayed with their unit, more than one year, but duplicated themselves with another person taking on the class the following year.

Eventually, that teacher was to move onto the next unit, having taken all five units with the opportunity to recycle, in order to really get the lessons under their belts. Unfortunately, this never happened. As we were torn inwardly with the "John and James" scenario, where there were those jockeying to lead rather than follow the vision of the Pastor who established the following schedule:

- 6:00 P.M. Dinner
- 6:45 P.M. Devotions and Offering
- 7:00 P.M. Class time
- 7.45 P.M. Reassemble and departure

The schedule worked well for the first eight to ten years, but began to dwindle due to a loss of enthusiasm and ongoing vision.

The Church is Air Conditioned

The problem of cooling off the church during the summer months was addressed many times. Due to a dome in the ceiling of the sanctuary, the head of the Trustee Board said that the church could never be air conditioned because it would be too expensive.

However, we moved forward, thanks to Deaconess Lurleen Chesson who said in very convincing words, "Pastor, yes we can. We women will air condition this church if you let us." Reverend Jones shared with me how he installed a new cooling system in Bethany Baptist, and recommended his contractor to me. After the contractor's visit, he determined that he could air condition the three floors for $80,000. We worked up a plan and the job was done.

We also installed a new bathroom for the women parishioners of the church. The new women's bathroom was installed in a hidden space downstairs beside the men's room, which was in a location we never considered. It turned out to be much larger and conveniently accommodated a greater number of women from the church. Now that I reflect, it is amazing to me how St. John's operated with only one upstairs bathroom for nearly 85 years, with the women having to climb a long stairway up to a third floor bathroom. Thanks be to God, we got it done and the new downstairs ladies' room was added.

Chair Glide

We purchased a chair glide due to the steep steps leading up to the church's entranceway. With the assistance of the chair glide, older ladies of the church didn't have the task of climbing steps. They entered the walkway on the side of the church, through the downstairs lobby and rode the chair glide up to the sanctuary floor. Thus, this eliminated having to climb any steps at all.

Dream of a New Sanctuary

Following the Church's 90th Anniversary, Deacon John Shipp, chairman of the deacon board made a brilliant suggestion. He recommended that the church should use the proceeds from the 90th Church Anniversary to begin making plans for a new edifice.

The first idea was to renovate the existing sanctuary at 448 West 152nd Street, but we ran into a problem because the edifice had landmark status. We couldn't change the façade, according to the Landmark Commission of New York City. So the next idea was to renovate our Community Center across the street, as renovating the church caused quite a stir of emotions for the members and me. We never realized how attached we were to the old church building, nor did we consider that the Center across the street (459 West 162nd) would give us more options with which to work.

After much comparison, the majority moved to renovate across the street and turn the old three story building in our multipurpose community center. The problem was how we were going to raise about two and a half to three million dollars to have a modern, "user-friendly" new edifice.

The Reverend Robert Perry, Pastor of Union Baptist Church in Stanford, Connecticut gave us our answer. He was quite a leader and had just finished erecting his new edifice in Stanford. He sent us his fund raising plans in order for us to develop a way that we could raise the money,

Generis

Following the morning services one Sunday, we were able to obtain the lead trainer, Herman Johnson of the Generis Organization in Atlanta, who came and met with us. The members liked the idea. Therefore, we signed a three year contract whereby a training program was conducted and projected. Hopefully, at the end of the three years we would have the money or thereabouts.

In the second year of 2008, when the economy began to decline, the officers got anxious because the funds began to dwindle. Each Sunday there were two baskets, one for our regular tithes and the other for the new building. The people committed to giving the total amount and to give it proportionately per person, with the theme, "Not Equal Amount but Equal Sacrifice."

Air Rights

Although the fund raising dwindled to a trickle, we still raised separate money for the building fund. However, we also needed to obtain a capital improvement loan for the remainder.

Several realtors contacted us with the idea of paying a certain dollar amount for the "air space" above the community center. Air space is the space above the roof, and real estate developers buy the space in order to build high rise apartments or condos for real estate purposes. This is where we are now, and if this comes through, we will be on our way which is our prayer.

Gentrification

The neighborhood of Hamilton Heights in West Harlem is no longer just a Black community. Whites have moved in in droves, which has caused the rent s to quadruple in the last ten years. The brownstone prices have multiplied ten to twelve times more than they were ten years ago, tempting the heirs of original homeowners to sell and forsake their community. So what we are looking at is a dwindling Black p opulation and a rising "yuppie" population that is traditionally "un-churched." The challenge is whether the Gospel can cross the lines of race and culture, because there is also the cultural divide or a rapidly rising "Hispanic p opulation."

The Harlem of Old

It is not white flight any longer. Due to the current shift in population, we will never know the tumultuous Harlem of old. Only a remnant remains of the religious and cultural *Mecca* that once was the capital of the Black world or the heart of Black Culture.

When I walk the streets of Harlem, the old people I knew when I first arrived are all dead, and their children are now the elders. Many of the children no longer live in the apartments they grew up in, because the landlords have sold out to the yuppie bidders for more money. Hence,

Harlem is changing again, this time dislocating Blacks who fought so hard to settle here.

I am reminded as I walk uptown on Eight Avenue beginning at 116th Street, and the surrounding areas, that I once literally held my breath with fear as I travelled along that street. And that was less than twenty years ago. Now three-or four-story high risers stand where the tenements were located, and lunch is served during the summer on 145th Street and Bradhurst Avenue at the old Colonial Park, now known as the Jackie Robinson Park. Perhaps you will say this is a good thing. However, people have been dislocated from their homes due to the growing number of high risers in Harlem, chicken franchises, McDonalds, large franchises like Starbucks and the establishment of fancy restaurants and/or sidewalk cafes. All of this has out priced the average Harlemite, many of whom are returning to the South and the Caribbean.

CHAPTER SEVENTEEN

FINAL THOUGHTS

As I look back over my years at my journey of faith, I must admit that my Harlem journey has been a miraculous and marvelous one, filled with faith and trust in God.

Although Daddy didn't show any feeling or excitement for my success, regardless of his demeanor, I am confident he would have been pleased with my accomplishments and the knowledge that I adapted his philosophy on independence. Just imagine, I moved from the small town of Ahoskie, North Carolina and settled in Harlem even though I was warned I might not survive in Harlem. Yet, in October 2012, I was the Senior Pastor of John's Baptist Church for forty years.

I married Minnie Watts in 1972 and have fathered three sons. Our first son John, Jr., was born in 1975. He is a law partner with one of the largest international law firms in the world. His accomplishments are possible because he attended Columbia University Undergraduate School and studied with Jack Greenburg who was the Dean and a former Supreme Court Nominee. He is a graduate of Fordham University Law School and is married to Rochelle Brutus, M.D. who is a psychiatrist. They are the parents of a five year daughter, Camryn and three year old son, Ethan.

Our second son James Augustus was born in 1976. He graduated from George Washington University with honors and Downstate Medical

College in Brooklyn. In 2010, he was the first African-American, Chief of Obstetrics at North Shore Hospital to hold this position. He is now an Obstetrician at a leading facility in Corning, New York.

My third son Jerome Sharif was born in 1979 and was considered a boy wonder in elementary, junior and high school. He enrolled at Hampton University as a pre–med student, transferred to George Washington University for his sophomore year, Mercy College for his third year and Lehman College for the fourth year. He presently works as a Supervisor of Environmental Services for a hospital in the New York area.

Minnie was first a Day Care teacher part time until John, four and James, three enrolled in Day Care. After Jerome the youngest was born, she returned to college and earned a Master's Degree from Lehman College and became a First Grade Elementary School teacher. She eventually became a *reading* specialist for her school. Minnie also frequently performs as the star soloist in the Inspirational church Choir. We have both received numerous citations, awards and certificates in the area of church and community service.

Praises go to my wife who has been the "glue" that has held the family together.

It has been quite an "amazing" journey, from the family farm of Quankey, North Carolina to one of the leading churches in New York State and the nation. To God be the glory for the things He has done in my life. His Amazing Grace, is displayed and manifested in my life from "Once dead' physically, but brought back to life by the power and the grace of God and the prayers of an old mid wife, by the name of Miss Mary Manley. This has indeed been a long and amazing journey because I got here by trusting in God and in His Holy Word.

Glossary of Names

Rev. Ralph W. Abernathy, V.P., Southern Christian Leadership Conference (S.C.L.C.). 6, 49, 71, 97,108, 111,117

Saul Alinsky, Organizer, Strike Against Kodak, Rochester, New York. 144

Dr. Samuel Austin, President, Empire Missionary Baptist State Convention, N.Y. 159

Rev. Wm. R. Bailey, Pastor, Calvary Baptist Church, East Orange, N.J. 6, 32,33, 39, 113

Mrs. Alice Balance, Organizer, Bertie County, North Carolina 81

Dr. J. Pius Barbour, Pastor, Calvary Baptist Church, Chester, P.A. 6, 43, 133

Styron Barnes, Merchant, Williamston, North Carolina 54

Rev. David Billings, Chair, Board of Christian Education, St. John's Baptist, N.Y. 117

Rev. P.A. Bishop, Pastor, Hertford County, New Carolina 83

Mr. Blanton, Admin. Roanoke Chowon Hospital, Ahoskie, North Carolina 43, 85, 86

Ben Branch, Saxophonist, Bread Basket Choir, Chicago, Illinois 101

Carlos Brown, Insurance Agent, North Carolina Mutual, Winton, N.C. 6, 52, 55, 60, 83, 86

E. P. Brown President, Georgia Pacific Lumber Co., Murfreesboro, N.C. 86

James Brown, Rock-N-Roll Singer, (Godfather of Soul) 15, 71,103, 111

Rev. Dr. Jesse Brown, Old Testament Professor, Crozer Theological Seminary, Chester, PA. 41, 43

Mrs. Irene Yates, School Teacher, R.L. Vann High School, Ahoskie, North Carolina 62

Rev. Johnny Youngblood, Pastor, St. Paul Baptist Church/President Nehemiah Housing Project, Brooklyn, New York 6, 144

Mrs. Sarah Yearbin, Organizer, North Carolina Fund, Durham, North Carolina 78

ABOUT THE AUTHOR

Dr. Barbara Eleanor Adams teaches English at the College of New Rochelle–School of New Resources, in New York. She is the author of *Dr. John Henrik Clarke: Master Teacher*, *Dr. John Henrik Clarke: The Early Years*, and was a contributing author to *The Encyclopedia of Black Studies*. Dr. Adams is the retired Director of the College of New Rochelle Rosa Parks Campus in Harlem, New York. She resides in Harlem, New York.